"GILLIAN, NO ONE way before," Steven said quietly.

"How?" she asked.

"So . . . I don't know . . . mindless, I suppose."

"I hope I make you feel other things too."

"Oh, you do. How you *do* do that!"

"Tell me," she demanded.

"You're shameless," he said. "Shall I count the ways?"

"Elizabeth Barrett Browning," she said gleefully. "You surprise me."

"All us jocks are illiterate?"

"It's just that you never seem to have time for—" She paused. "So tell me, how do I make you feel?"

"I would rather show than tell," he said with a taunting smile.

"That's cheati—" The last of her words was stopped by his lips. Gillian decided she preferred that too. . . .

WHAT ARE *LOVESWEPT* ROMANCES?

They are stories of true romance and touching emotion. We believe those two very important ingredients are constants in our highly sensual and very believable stories in the LOVE-SWEPT line. Our goal is to give you, the reader, stories of consistently high quality that may sometimes make you laugh, sometimes make you cry, but are always fresh and creative and contain many delightful surprises within their pages.

Most romance fans read an enormous number of books. Those they truly love, they keep. Others may be traded with friends and soon forgotten. We hope that each LOVESWEPT romance will be a treasure—a "keeper." We will always try to publish

LOVE STORIES YOU'LL NEVER FORGET
BY AUTHORS YOU'LL ALWAYS REMEMBER

The Editors

Loveswept ® 746

IMPETUOUS

PATRICIA POTTER

BANTAM BOOKS
NEW YORK · TORONTO · LONDON · SYDNEY · AUCKLAND

IMPETUOUS

A Bantam Book / July 1995

If you would be interested in receiving protective vinyl covers for your Loveswept books, please write to this address for information:

Loveswept
Bantam Books
P.O. Box 985
Hicksville, NY 11802

ISBN 0-553-44194-9

Published simultaneously in the United States and Canada

ONE

Steven Morrow slammed his hand down on his desk, unable to control his anger.

Just two weeks before the grand opening of his new real estate development, and Leslie Turner, the woman handling its promotion, had been called out of town on an emergency. This morning, Gillian Collins, her partner in their public relations firm Word Shop, had called him to say she was taking over and would be coming by later that day.

Steven had talked to a number of agencies before choosing Word Shop because of its impeccable reputation and because Leslie seemed to understand him and what he was trying to do with Cherokee Hills. All that careful selection was turning out to have been for nothing.

Gillian Collins did not fill him with confidence. Her irreverent sense of humor had rubbed him the wrong way the first time they met, and he wondered whether she ever took anything seriously. He would make sure she took Cherokee Hills seriously, dammit.

His intercom buzzed, and his secretary told him Gillian Collins had arrived. Instead of having her sent in, he strode impatiently over to the door and opened it.

Steven took one look at Gillian and silently cursed. If there were ever two more disparate people than Gillian and her partner, he'd never met them. Where Leslie made him think of still waters that run deep, Gillian was like a neon sign at night. He'd learned about flash the hard way, and he'd steered a good distance from it ever since. But according to Leslie, Gillian's work was superb. She had been the creative source of the marketing program for the houses in Cherokee Hills. The ads had been a bit too showy for his taste, but Leslie had said, "Trust us." He had—and they'd sold homes.

Still, he couldn't help feeling resentful of being saddled with Gillian at the last minute. Too late now though to change agencies.

"Miss Collins," he said stiffly.

"Mr. Morrow," she replied with what Steven would have sworn was mockery in her voice. His back went up, like a wild animal sensing an enemy.

"Come in," he said curtly, holding the door open and then closing it with a little more force than necessary after she'd entered, portfolio in hand.

He turned quickly enough to catch the pained expression on her face. But it immediately disappeared into a wide smile.

"How long will Leslie be gone?"

"I'm not sure."

"She *will* be back for the opening." It was a statement, not a question.

She shrugged. "Everything will be fine. She has everything ready. The ads, the catering, the brochure." Her smile grew even wider, which for some reason, made him suspicious.

He sat on the corner of his desk and studied her, just as he studied subcontractors when he wished to intimidate them. It didn't seem to work. She'd already seated herself and looked entirely at ease.

There was no reason for his antipathy. While Gillian never appeared overjoyed to see him, neither had she ever been anything but cordial. But the bright colors she always wore seemed a bit unprofessional. She looked more like a gypsy with her gleaming, almost black hair, laughing dark brown eyes, large hoop earrings, red silk blouse, and black skirt trimmed with red and gold. She was like an exotic butterfly, one he might someday try to catch. . . .

Damn. His mind was moving away from business. It never did that. Never.

"How familiar are you with Cherokee Hills?" he finally asked.

"I went there with Leslie when we first got the account. It's . . . nice."

"Nice?" He was outraged. Cherokee Hills was a meticulously planned development of several neighborhoods spread over five hundred acres of rolling hills, with carefully sited parks, including a championship golf course and country club. It was everything he had dreamed of as a child. And more.

"*Very* nice," she amended, as Steven glared at her.

Her attempt to mollify him was offset by the unrepentent twinkle in her eyes, as if she enjoyed baiting him. Then the twinkle turned into a laser beam directed at the core of him, penetrating, looking for clues. He sure as hell didn't want this kind of scrutiny.

"Do you have the acceptances for the golf tournament?" he asked, more tersely than he'd intended.

She pulled out a list of people who had RSVP'ed for the celebrity golf tournament, the principal attraction of the opening. The governor was on the list, which was a tremendous coup. So were two television anchormen, three former Falcon football stars, seven baseball players from the Atlanta Braves, and several members of the Atlanta Hawks basketball team. There was also a very well-known actor from a television series being filmed in Atlanta. Proceeds from the event were to go to the local children's hospital, and that had helped attract participants.

Steven's own past helped too. Few people forgot that he had been an all-star football player at the University of Georgia, that he just missed receiving the Heisman Trophy in his junior year. It was a past he hated to trade upon, but for Cherokee Hills he would sell his soul.

As his gaze ran down the list, he felt her eyes bore in on him again. Suddenly, surprisingly, the room grew too warm for him.

"Mr. Morrow?" His eyes met hers, and there was a clash of wills. Anticipation rippled up his spine.

"Yes, Miss Collins?" he asked with exaggerated politeness.

Gillian hesitated. She had studied all of Leslie's plans for the grand opening for the last two days, and one thing was missing. The golf tournament was to benefit children, so there should be children at the opening. But what kid wanted to see a bunch of adults hit little balls around all day?

"I have an idea," she said finally, "to sort of expand the activities, but first I have to check and see whether it can be done."

"May I have a hint?"

She grinned, and the hoop earrings danced attractively against the dark hair. "Tomorrow. Can I call you tomorrow about it?"

He walked to his chair behind the desk. The latter was large enough for blueprints, and for intimidating visitors. "I think Leslie has done a capable job. I don't think we need anything else." He realized, as he spoke, that he probably sounded stuffy, but he didn't need any more changes. He ran his fingers through his hair, as he sometimes did when uncertain. He hated that feeling, and it didn't make him charitable toward the woman in front of him.

"Please," she said. "And then if you don't like the idea you can squelch it."

Something in her eyes made a negative answer impossible. Hell, he could just say no tomorrow. And after hearing her idea, he could probably reject it with

good reason. He looked down at his calendar. "The only time I have open tomorrow is late afternoon."

"Five? Six?"

He was being steamrollered, and he wasn't happy about it. Agreement seemed the best way to get rid of her. "Six," he said.

They quickly went over a few more things: The final proof for a one-page newspaper ad planned for this weekend, approval of radio spots that would be snowing Atlanta for four days prior to the opening.

Everything about the opening had to project an image of quality. Steven was determined there would be no mistakes. Thank God, Leslie had already done much of the work in the past three months. He could rely on Leslie's good sense. He wasn't so sure about her partner's.

Finally, Gillian was ready to go. She stood up, then grinned at him. "Six," she said as if she knew he was testing her resolve by making their appointment so late.

Now *she* was testing *his* resolve. But he had learned control long ago—control of his own feelings, of his own reactions. He hated any assault on it, feared the consequences. And he certainly didn't like Gillian Collins for making even the slightest crack in it.

"Six," he reaffirmed. "But I don't think I'll change my mind."

It was a challenge, pure and simple. She was wasting her time and effort, he was warning her.

But she merely smiled back with mock patience. Well, Steven thought, she didn't know him very well.

Irritated with himself, with the way that irrepressible smile did things inside he didn't appreciate, he abruptly stood up and strode to the door, holding it open for her.

As she brushed against him, his hand accidentally touched hers. He felt rare electric sensation at the contact that seemed to run through his body. She turned to regard him for a moment, and he had the strangest feeling that she was as disconcerted as he was. There was a momentary confusion in her eyes, even as the gleam persisted.

"Six," she repeated, her voice softer than it had been during their conversation, and turned and walked away before he could answer.

Stunned by his strange reaction to her, he found himself watching her as she left the office. His lips twisted slightly upward in a rare grin as she seemed to bounce, not walk, to the outer door. She looked very nice from his position, her back straight, but her body movements full of confidence and energy and an enticing swing.

Steven caught his secretary's surprised expression, and he restrained his smile. *That* was the last thing he should be thinking of at the moment.

But after she left, he couldn't quite focus his mind on the other problems on his plate. He kept seeing that mischievous smile and beguiling walk. He was only worried, he told himself, about whatever scheme she was considering.

So why then did those attractively expressive dark eyes linger in his thoughts?

Hours after she left, he found himself staring out the window of his small modest office. So much depended on the success of Cherokee Hills. He had poured every penny of his own money in the project and called in every I.O.U. He'd stretched his credit to the limit, and had lived little better than a monk for the past few years. His hand tightened around the pencil he had been fingering, and he felt it break in his hands.

The flashes were coming again, the images, like an old nickelodeon, flickering in rapid movement across his brain. The soul-crunching violence, the fists, the blood. So much blood that last time.

Control, he told himself. He had lost that tight control of himself, of events, in the past hours. Dammit, that's why they were coming again, those memories that never entirely left him, that kept driving him. Slowly, so damned slowly, he finally forced the scenes from his mind and once more locked them away.

Gillian left Cherokee Hills Development Corporation offices like a saint given an assignment to save a sinner. Full of righteous enthusiasm.

She had an idea. Boy, did she have an idea!

Lights had flashed, lightning had struck, bulbs had exploded inside her head as she'd talked to Steven Morrow. Ideas came to her that way. Not in little whispers, but in great revelations.

If only she could convince Steven Morrow.

She sensed it would not be easy.

She thought back to the work session, and to the cool gray eyes and unsmiling face. He was not a man for frivolity. He would have to be convinced by hard, cold facts, and that was why she hadn't sprung her brainstorm on him. She didn't want a no yet. She wanted time to develop an unarguable case.

Gillian stepped into her small red sports car, her one luxury. It was an older model, and it hadn't cost that much originally, but the upkeep was horrendous. Nonetheless, it gave her a sense of freedom and individuality that was worth every cent.

Her mind rapidly ran over her plan, and she nearly wriggled with excitement. She could possibly pull off the greatest event in Atlanta public relations history, help a stranded Russian circus, and even might, just might, make Steve Morrow crack a smile.

Suddenly that was important, though she didn't know why.

She'd winced when Leslie had called from Chicago yesterday and told her she was staying for several days with her new fiancé, the Scot folksinger who, in a matter of two weeks, had turned her from a cautious never-get-involved-again professional into a spontaneous madly-in-love woman.

It had meant, of course, that Gillian had to take over the Cherokee Hills project, and she'd never cared much for Steven Morrow. Even his use of the name, Steven, instead of Steve seemed to signify yuppiedom to her. Pretentiousness. So unlike most of her clients, usually folks in show business or entertainment: Nightclubs, promoters, musicians. They were night people, like her, and she enjoyed their usually optimistic view of life. You had to be optimistic in show business to survive.

But she had forced a Scots folksinger on Leslie, and now Leslie, in turn, was forcing Steven Morrow on her, and she would do her best, just as Leslie had. That, however, was where the similarity would end. She had no desire to fall in love, particularly with an uptight developer. Even the thought gave her cold shivers.

Or *was* it that thought?

She remembered that brief contact in the office, the way her knees suddenly weakened in such an odd way. It didn't make sense. She didn't even like the man.

But she would like to see him smile, just once. He would probably be quite attractive if he did. Heck, she knew he would, with that slightly mussed sandy hair and strong, craggy features.

She knew just the people to make him smile, if he would give her a chance.

TWO

"Miss Gilly!"

A voice boomed out before a large bearlike man swept her up in a hug and kissed each cheek, first left, then right. "We are sooo greatly thanks to you."

Gillian did her best to unwind herself from the embrace and stood back, grinning at Sergei Chukov, the ringmaster and leader of the Stars of Russia Circus.

Gillian was soon surrounded by a growing group of performers dressed in everything from tights to sweat suits. They chattered away in Russian, but basically Gilly sensed they were saying thank you in their own particularly boisterous way.

A dog barked until someone commanded it to stop. The dog did so. Immediately. But the sound of excited, fulsome voices didn't abate.

"They've arrived!" she said, not hiding her triumph. Gillian had returned two days earlier from her self-imposed mission to free the circus animals from impoundment or worse.

Sergei beamed. "All. So many thanks to you. My Natasha, she is so glad to have her babies. And Alexei, he has his Romeo. They have been . . . what is it in English . . . not to let go?"

"Inseparable," Gillian offered.

"That's it." Sergei beamed. "My English, it will be so good by when we leave." His face lost its glow, and little lines formed around his eyes. "You have hear no more from the government?"

Gillian shook her head. The Stars of Russia Circus had landed in Atlanta four weeks earlier, only to be abandoned by their promoters and financiers, leaving a trail of debts behind them. The circus was broke, and so were all the performers who pooled what little money they'd had after the disaster. But that was mostly gone now, and there seemed to be no assistance anywhere. The Russian government said it couldn't help. The State Department said they had no funds to send a Russian circus home.

They had not even paid the bills in Boston, the last city in which the circus performed prior to coming to Atlanta. The promoters had done no promoting, no advertising, and consequently few attended the performances. The circus animals were seized by officials in Boston after an unpaid hotel filed a complaint.

The circus was supposed to perform in Atlanta but when its members arrived, they found no hotel, no salaries, and no animals. It was only then they'd learned they had been abandoned, and no one knew what to do with them.

It had become a cause célèbre in Atlanta, with endless news stories and television reports, but no one came forward to help in any substantial way. No one but a suburban motel owner who said the performers could stay there free, and a fast-food chicken franchise and an Italian restaurant who kept them supplied in pizza and fried chicken.

And Gillian. Gillian had read about the circus and went to see for herself. When she had heard about the animals, the animal lover inside her had become very indignant. And an indignant Gillian was a force to be reckoned with. Gillian was only too aware of that weakness of hers. She lost all perspective when she felt someone was being taken advantage of, or mistreated. Sloughing off her business responsibilities on her partner, Gillian had flown to Boston and, after a week of media blackmail, promises of great public relations and goodwill benefits, and all the charm she could muster, won the release of ten trick dogs, a chimpanzee, six white horses, and a trained bear. Then, she'd discovered that the trucks carrying the animals had left, also without being paid. With pledges of super publicity, she talked officials of an airline into transporting all the animals for free.

She had rescued the animals, but she still didn't know how to get Sergei and his circus family home, and she'd taken that feat on as a personal crusade. Trouble was, money was tight everywhere, and a Russian circus was apparently last on everyone's charity list.

Gillian knew she was a sucker for a sad story, and sad eyes. That was why she had a stray dog and a half-blind cat no one else would take. And if there was anything sadder than an unwanted animal, it was the combined large expressive eyes of abandoned Russian circus performers. She had thought about submitting that particular observation to *The Guinness Book of World Records.*

They had been so expressive, in fact, that she had dropped everything and temporarily abandoned her own business to go free the animals.

And now she was paying the price. Her good deed had thrown her personal client, a Scottish folksinger named Connor MacLaren, together with her partner, Leslie. Who would have ever thought they would fall in love in one week? And run away from home.

Despite the gravity of the situation, Gillian had to smile. She smiled every time she thought of Leslie and Connor. Even if they also made her feel a trifle sad and even a bit envious. They seemed so happy.

But it had also meant that Leslie had left her to deal with Steven Morrow, and his grand opening. Real estate. Golf tournaments. Politicians. Yuck.

Which was why she was here, she reminded herself. She drew Sergei off into one of the few quiet places on motel grounds otherwise alive with exercising and performing circus stars.

"I have an idea," she told him, and saw his face brighten, the dark, soulful eyes come alive.

"You do so much always," he said, and Gillian had to grin at the now familiar mishmash of words.

As she started to speak, a chimpanzee suddenly whirled itself at her, jumping up in her arms and giving her a big swipe of the tongue. She had become his friend in Boston when he was pining away in a tiny cage.

"He is well?" she asked the beaming Ukrainian who had just approached. The man uttered a few unrecognizable words, and Sergei grinned at her.

"Alexei wants to know if you will marry him?"

"He's that grateful?" Gillian retorted.

"He says you are beautiful . . . and kind."

Gillian thought fast. "Tell him thank you, but I have a fiancé."

As Sergei translated, the chimp's owner gave her a soulful look, and grabbed her hand, kissing it passionately before spouting a number of additional words.

"He says he is . . . how do you say in English, very tragic?"

"Sad," Gillian said. "I think only sad."

Alexei finally left after kissing her hand mournfully, and Gillian spoke with Sergei about the possibility of performing at the grand opening where the governor and other influential people, including the media, would be.

"Yes, yes," he said. "This is what we need. To perform. Thank you, Miss Gilly. Thank you."

Gillian shook her head. "It's not certain yet."

"Ah, but it shall be. Miss Gilly do all things." He kissed her again on both cheeks. Enthusiastically.

Right where the chimp had preceded him. "I go tell others."

Gillian watched fatalistically as the circus ringmaster called the others together to give what she knew was his version of the conversation. Total optimism. In a moment she would be surrounded again by ebullient Russians. She decided to leave. While she could.

She had a gut feeling she was right.

Steve Morrow and his grand opening. He needed life, children, enthusiasm.

Sergei needed an audience, and a financial angel.

They were meant for each other.

But Steven Morrow was a challenge. Ex-jock turned uptight businessman. Probably an ultra conservative. Together with an abandoned Russian circus?

She had her work cut out for her.

Steven Morrow found himself doodling. He never doodled. He never did anything that wasn't necessary. Not for the past few years anyway. He had spent altogether too much time doing that earlier.

He remembered, in fact, doodling a lot in classes when he played quarterback in college. Education had not seemed important then. He was going on to the pros, and he'd spent class time designing football plays, not business plans. It was a miscalculation he'd never stopped regretting.

Steven stared up at the spot where his Most Valuable Player plaques decorated the walls. He disliked them intensely! They reminded him of failure, not success. But they impressed bankers, investors, and clients.

He'd never understood why an over-the-hill crippled football player was impressive for the fact alone that he'd once had some success as a quarterback in college. But he'd stopped trying to figure that out a long time ago. The fact remained that his sports career was his most important asset, not the fact that he was painstakingly developing one of the finest communities in Atlanta.

Perhaps that was why Gillian had startled him. She was obviously not in awe of his athletic reputation. The opposite, in fact. It was, in a way, refreshing. In another, disconcerting.

He looked down at his watch. Five forty-five. He was restless. But then he was usually restless. His working days presently lasted twelve to fourteen hours, sometimes longer, but then he thrived on pure adrenaline. He always had.

Steven heard the outer door to his office open, and stood, stretching his long form and flexing his bad leg. It usually ached at this time of day, reminding him of the sack that ruined his football career, his chances for a pro career and landed him in a hospital for months. It took all his will not to limp as he moved toward the door of his office, but he had long ago determined not to let his injury affect him more than it already had.

If Gillian Collins had reminded him of a neon sign yesterday, she was like a nova today. She wore a yellow peasant-style blouse and a gold skirt, a combination that might look garish on someone else, but on Gillian it looked spectacular. She wore the same gold hoop earrings against shining dark hair, and her mouth flashed the same bright smile as yesterday. A challenging mockery, however, danced in her eyes, and suddenly, unexpectedly, he anticipated a pleasant battle.

He raised an eyebrow in question. "Miss Collins?"

She grinned. "Gillian. Or Gilly if you prefer."

"Gillian," he decided gravely. "You have something to show me?"

Gillian looked down at the portfolio she carried. "Yep."

"Let's see it!" He knew he was abrupt, but then he was always abrupt these days.

Gillian tipped her head up inquisitively. "It will take a while."

Steven looked down at his watch. "Would you like to talk about it during dinner? I haven't had anything to eat all day." He watched as her eyes suddenly seemed to gleam in a way that fascinated him.

She nodded, and he rolled down his shirtsleeves which had been pushed up past his elbows and ran his fingers through his hair. He wasn't wearing a coat or tie; he seldom did unless completely necessary. "Let's go."

He took her arm and guided her forcefully out the door, turning out the light behind him and closing his office door. He did the same with the outer office, and then they were outside. He steered her easily to a dark blue pickup truck, his glance searching and finding a small red sports car now sitting alone outside his office. His mouth twisted in a way no one could call a smile. "Sorry about the transportation," but the words were obviously just mouthed and not really meant. He didn't sound sorry at all.

At the steep step of the pickup, Gillian took his proffered hand and was nearly catapulted into the seat. When he'd moved around the truck and into his own seat, she was still feeling the effortless strength with which he'd propelled her into the seat. She looked over at him and observed dryly, "You should have been a tackle."

Gillian saw him wince slightly but didn't say anything. The truck, however, started with a jerk before moving into the road. His eyes were firmly set ahead.

Gillian shifted against the door where she could have a better view of him. Too bad his personality resembled Grumpy in Snow White because, on looks alone, he would make a passable Prince Charming.

His hair was sandy blond, not curly exactly, but thick and tousled, apparently from running fingers through it. Before he'd smoothed his sleeves down, she'd had a great view of muscled forearms and tanned skin with a feathery dusting of blond hairs. His hands looked strong and capable as they moved easily along the straight shift and steered the truck with indifferent ease.

His face was arresting, strong and arrogant, and saved from perfection by a nose which had obviously been broken more than once. There was also a thin scar up the side of his face, and she remember the grave, watchful gray eyes that had warily scanned her yesterday.

Gillian also recalled that strange impulse yesterday, an almost compelling need to make him laugh. And that feeling returned now. She was shocked at how strong it was.

She didn't even like him. Maybe she just wanted to discover whether he could smile or not. An intellectual exercise, she told herself.

"Well?"

His one word broke her thought like a hammer shattered glass. She looked up guiltily.

"Your idea? What is it?"

Gillian swallowed her natural honesty and started diplomatically. That was something she'd learned painstakingly from Leslie. To be diplomatic under the most provoking of circumstances. "The golf tournament is . . . very nice, but . . ."

"There's that word again," he said. "Nice. You have a way of making it not quite a compliment." His tone had a warning edge to it.

"But," she hurried on, "we can add another really nice . . . ah . . . wonderful touch. Something for children. And for some of the women who don't care for golf."

"There's a tennis demonstration. Open house and refreshments," he said stiffly. "Sports celebrities . . ."

Demonstration, chemonstration, Gillian wanted to throw back. Who cared? There were other people in the world except jocks. People who liked circuses.

"You also have beautiful woods and hills and some really . . . fine homes," she said. "And Cherokee

Hills needs a lot of publicity, not just in the sports section."

"Leslie thought the plans were just fine." His voice was coldly firm.

Gillian started counting to ten. Leslie and she had been successful because they complemented each other. They had been most productive on the campaigns they had planned together because they both brought something different to the final product: Leslie's reason and way with words, and Gillian's imagination and art design. But they had not worked together on this one. Gillian had been very busy when Leslie was working on Cherokee Hills, and then the development hadn't really interested her.

But now, by default, it was *hers*.

And she knew this idea of hers would work. She felt it in her bones, and her bones had always been right.

But before she could say anything, he had driven into a small shopping center, stopping before a dimly lighted Italian restaurant. "I hope you like Italian food."

It was a statement, not a question, and Gillian felt she was being tested in some way. It was not a feeling she liked. But she simply nodded in the same cool way, not admitting she loved Italian food.

She didn't wait for him to come around to her side of the door. It was not, after all, a social outing, but a business meeting. Nonetheless when he met her at the front of the truck, his hand went to her shoulder in such a natural way that she knew he was used to taking control. An unexpected warmth crept up her skin from the spot he touched.

"Signor Morrow," a man in a shiny black suit greeted him, "and Signorina." He beamed at them both.

"The usual table," Steven said easily, and they were guided to a small table adjacent to a wall of windows overlooking the parking lot. It was the best lit table in the dim restaurant, and Gillian suddenly wondered if he brought work here. For some reason, her gaze went to his ring finger and found it bare. She didn't understand why she'd bothered.

As they sat down, she tried to remember everything Leslie had said about Steven Morrow. She'd talked about the quality of the development. She'd talked about how Steven knew exactly what he wanted in the grand opening. And although Gillian had thought him cold the few times she'd met him, she knew Leslie liked and admired him. But then Leslie liked nearly everyone.

She looked up and found the subject of her thoughts studying her as if she were a biology specimen. Gillian wondered momentarily how anyone could have such enigmatic eyes. They were a beautiful silver gray, and she imagined the color deepened with his emotions. If he ever had any.

"Would you like a glass of wine?"

Yes. She needed one. She didn't understand why she was feeling like the contents of her health drink mixture as various fruits were being pulverized. "No, thank you," she said instead. She needed all her senses.

"A glass of your burgundy for me," he told the waiter, "and the lady will have . . ." He turned toward her.

"Iced tea," she said unenthusiastically, desperately wanting the burgundy instead.

The side of his mouth twisted as if he knew exactly what she was thinking. Oh hell, she thought, almost changing her mind and then deciding she didn't want to give him that satisfaction.

After they'd ordered—lasagna for her and spaghetti for him—Gillian picked up her briefcase, opened it, and took out a sketch for an advertisement she'd completed just before coming.

There was the entrance to Cherokee Hills, and the headline: "Come experience the magic of Cherokee Hills." The ad was composed of four theater stages, a master of ceremonies pulling at the curtain of each. In the center of one was a golfer teeing off; in another a man was raising a tennis racket as though he'd just won; in the third a family was picnicking under a great oak tree; and in the fourth, graceful riders stood balanced on two white horses as a playful clown with a chimp looked on.

At the bottom: "A day of enchantment for the entire family."

She watched as his eyes skimmed over the copy. Without expression, he laid it down next to his plate. "I've already approved the advertising."

"And you never change your mind?" It was a challenge, pure and simple.

"Not often."

"I believe that," she retorted.

"And you don't approve?" It was a baiting type of question, and Gillian rose to it.

"Of rigidity? Not often," she shot back, anger replacing her hard-earned diplomacy. Back in her mind, she knew the Word Shop couldn't afford to lose this account, but she couldn't stop the words.

A bright gleam shone in his eyes, and his mouth twisted again in what might pass for the faintest smile. "How did you and Leslie ever get together?"

The switch in topic was so unexpected, it almost disarmed Gillian. Almost. It certainly surprised her. She tipped her head inquisitively. "Why?"

"You seem so different."

"Everyone's different," Gillian said.

"Ah, but some are more so than others."

"You're avoiding the subject."

"No, I'm not. Why do you want to change everything?"

"Because I think it would help the grand opening."

"Explain!"

"I thought I had. Expand the activities . . . and consequently the interest."

"I thought agencies liked to target their audience, not send out grapeshot."

"This *is* targeting. Families."

"It's the men who buy."

"It's the women who select."

The side of his mouth twisted again, and Gillian knew suddenly she was being baited once more. He was arguing for argument's sake, and her estimation of him rose. He was testing her, weighing her, judging whether she really knew what she was doing.

"Proposition," she said, challenging him right back. "Proposition: Most major decisions are made by husbands and wives together these days."

He didn't assent or dissent, simply raised an eyebrow.

"And," she continued, "mothers, fathers, too, are swayed by their children's welfare: Safety, education, happiness."

"Cherokee Hills offers that. Country club. Swimming. Special activities for children."

"Country club activities," Gillian said softly. "Structure."

"And that's bad?"

Gillian shrugged. "No, but they need something else too. Magic. Magic and imagination and just plain fun. Show them Cherokee Hills offers that too."

"How?"

"A circus."

"During the grand opening?" His voice was not at all promising.

"Sure."

"And how do we find an accommodating circus?"

"The stranded Russian circus," Gillian announced with quiet satisfaction.

Steven Morrow stared at her with those unfathomable gray eyes, and she hurried on. "You must be aware of the publicity the circus is getting. This would help both of you. It would give the circus a chance to perform, show what it can do, and also draw enormous crowds to Cherokee Hills."

Again, Gillian felt like that same specimen in the biology lab.

"A bankrupt circus is going to help Cherokee Hills?" There was nothing encouraging in his voice, more like an incredulous disbelief that she would even suggest such a thing.

"Think of it," she said. "Children would adore it. The press would be out in force. Perhaps there would be enough attention to somehow . . ."

She stopped as she saw the wary expression on his face. And her heart dropped at his next words. "Just who are you thinking about helping? Cherokee Hills or the circus?"

The arrival of food prevented any answer. And for a moment, she was glad. The question had stopped her momentarily. Where *did* her real interest lie. She didn't particularly like the answer which came too quickly.

But she was right. She knew it. The circus would be as good for Cherokee Hills as the publicity and exposure would be for the circus. But she had to put her thoughts in order first. There was something about those eyes of his which made her doubt her own instincts. And that was rare. She always ran with her instincts.

"Are you sure you won't have some burgundy?" he

said, cutting into her thoughts, obviously trying to shelve any more discussion for the moment.

"No," she said.

"No, you won't, or no, you're not sure?"

She smiled. She couldn't help it. He had such a solemn look on his face, and she wasn't certain whether he was teasing or not. She could usually read someone's eyes, their face, but Steven Morrow gave nothing away. Absolutely nothing. "No, I'm not sure," she said.

"Another glass," Steven said to the waiter. "But you're usually sure?"

"About what?" Gillian countered.

"About everything."

Gillian suddenly found herself on the defensive. "No, not really, but about this . . ."

"This can wait. We were talking about you."

"*You* were talking about me. I was talking about the circus . . ." Gillian persisted, wondering how the conversation had so derailed.

"After dinner," he insisted, looking toward the heaping plate of spaghetti set down before him. "Emilio has the best Italian food in Atlanta."

"You come here often."

He nodded. "I'm almost an honorary member of the family. But then it's close to my office. It's fast, and it's good."

"Practical," Gillian said.

"Practical," he agreed.

"And you like practical things." It was a statement, not a question.

"I like predictable things," he corrected.

"Always?"

Steven turned his head slightly, as if seriously considering the question. He was amazed at himself, batting words across the table like balls across a net. He still didn't know why he'd invited her to dinner. He usually dined alone, reading the paper as he ate. It was the only time during the day he relaxed.

But he was relaxed now. Far more than he'd been in a long time, and he didn't know why. This was a business meeting, nothing more. He had already resolved to say no to any new proposal. Plans were too far along for changes now, and he didn't want anything to go wrong with the opening. As he'd told her, he liked things to be predictable. Practical. Reliable.

He enjoyed looking at her, though. She was like a bright ray of sunshine in the fading fall day, the bright yellow of her blouse contrasting with a slight dusky quality of her skin. With her straight dark hair and tanned skin, she looked as if she had Native American blood. Or even Italian. Whatever it was, it was striking. So was the smile which came easily, even when it had a certain amount of mockery in it.

Steven knew it was not the malicious kind, but more of a teasing challenge. She had a smile in her eyes as well as on her mouth, and he found it almost impossible not to respond to her.

But business and pleasure never mixed well. Particularly in this instance. The practical side of him wished that Leslie was back; the emotional side, which he had compressed into a very small crease of his brain, did not. He found himself enjoying this dinner more than any he'd had for a long time.

However, he was still not going to change his plans.

"Always," he confirmed.

"No adventure?"

"I've had enough adventure to satisfy me."

"You can never have too much adventure."

His mouth turned up in a small, wry smile. "It depends on what kind, Miss Collins. When I was a boy it was an adventure to get enough food for my brothers and myself. I really don't care to repeat that."

"Is that why you don't want to take chances?"

"I *am* taking a very big chance with Cherokee Hills, Miss Collins. I'm just trying to limit the risk as much as possible."

"I thought you were going to call me Gillian."

"Gillian, then," he conceded, knowing exactly why he'd reverted to her surname. Distance. He needed distance between them.

Gillian finished the last of her dinner, and took some additional pages from the briefcase. "This is the number of inches in newspapers and the number of television minutes already devoted to the Russian circus in just the past week. The publicity of a performance at your opening, together with the governor's appearance and that of the sports celebrities will be tremendous. So will the goodwill. And the circus is willing to perform for free. We can even invite some of the patients or ex-patients from the children's hospital," Gillian rushed on before he could interrupt. "Will you at least think about it?"

Steven leaned back in his chair. "Miss Collins . . . Gillian . . . I've worked hard to establish a certain image for Cherokee Hills. Quality. Value. Nothing but the best. Our market is upper level professionals and managers, who are usually conservative in both financing and investing. I just can't see the opening, at which the governor will be present, being touted by clowns . . . like those who stand at the entrance of so many of the apartment developments."

"Not just clowns," Gillian argued, "but some of the best circus acts in the world. Cherokee Hills is promoting athletics. There are no finer athletes than some of these circus performers."

Steven shook his head slowly, even regretfully. He had never known it to be difficult to say no before. Now, he did, and it surprised him. He didn't want the light in her eyes to dim. And that surprised him even more.

"Will you at least go out with me tomorrow and watch them?"

Her head was tipped slightly, and dark hair fell partially over one eye. The challenge in her voice was gone, replaced by a plea that was nigh onto irresistible.

He sighed, mentally surrendering. He wondered whether it was because he suddenly didn't want to disappoint her.

The bill came then, and he paid it with a credit

card. "I have work to do," he said, somewhat abruptly, and went over to her chair, pulling it out for her.

He took her arm and felt the warmth of her skin, and he didn't want to let go. So he did. And then at the door, she turned and those large brown eyes searched his face. "Will you?"

He nodded, and she smiled, a gamin grin that lit her face, seemed to light the whole evening.

"And you'll keep an open mind?"

"Nope," he said cheerfully, and her grin widened.

"Yes, you will," she said confidently, and Steven had a terrible suspicion she might be right. It was a thought almost as terrifying as when he was told he wouldn't play football ever again.

That's ridiculous, he told himself. There could be no comparison. Yet, he had the strangest feeling he was about to lose control of his life once more, to be jerked off the path he had so carefully constructed.

And he didn't like that sensation. He didn't like it at all.

THREE

Gillian sighed as she walked into her home, a garage apartment which sat behind a grand old mansion in the Druid Hills area of Atlanta.

It was more of a cottage than an apartment, and she liked its coziness. She had often thought about buying a home, as Leslie had, but something about the permanence of a home disturbed her. She did not want to be establishment. She did not want to be a home owner and responsible for things like new roofs and repainting. It was easier to pick up the phone and call her landlady.

No Name, the cat, and Spenser, the fat dachshund, were waiting at the door for her. Free spirit or not, Gillian had found herself the reluctant owner of two beasts who severely hampered her dreams of someday being a wild goose, free and unencumbered. But both had been destined for the gas chamber, and Gillian, who did volunteer public relations work for the Humane Society, hadn't been able to resist them on visits to the facility.

She let Spenser out, knowing he would not dare go out of the confines of the yard. He was too grateful for a home to risk losing it. No Name, on the other hand, never went out, never even wanted to go out, and simply meowed for his dinner.

Gillian saw to their needs and then turned on Beethoven's Fifth Symphony and curled up in the giant beanbag chair she loved. She felt strangely disturbed by today's events, even a bit haunted by those steady gray eyes that revealed so little.

There had been some odd moments tonight at dinner, minutes of awareness, of a kind of connection between them that was startling in its improbability.

Startling because Steven Morrow was the kind of man Gillian usually avoided, even disliked. Cautious. Business oriented. Conservative.

Stuffy.

No. He wasn't stuffy. He might be a lot of things, but stuffy wasn't one of them, she suddenly realized. Not with the pickup truck or his apparent friendship with the Italian family who ran the restaurant, nor those few moments of banter during which he seemed to mock himself as well as her.

Reserved? Yes. Guarded, most definitely. Manageable. Most certainly no.

So how could she do exactly that?

And how could she make him smile?

◆——————◆

Gillian had the circus prepped before she and a very reluctant Steven Morrow arrived at the motel that housed the performers. She had suggested taking her car since it was such a beautiful day and after a brief pause Steven had agreed.

The dry, quiet humor of last night seemed a mirage this morning. Steven's face was grim, his eyes hooded.

"Good morning," she said with a cheery grin as he opened the door to her car.

He cast her a suspicious look, an eyebrow raised in a dubious gesture as if to tell her exactly what he thought of this outing today.

"Thank you, it will be," she said airily as if he had replied in kind.

The side of his mouth jerked upward for a tiny second and then returned to its stubborn set. Gillian felt a momentary victory.

The top was down on the red sports car, and Gillian felt the sun touch her skin and the wind blow through her long hair. It was a perfect Atlanta fall day, bright and clear and warm with a comfortable breeze that teased the senses. She loved fall best of all seasons, the lazy laid-back mood it seemed to create with its smoky scent and drifting leaves.

But her passenger looked distinctly uncomfortable, as if he wasn't sure how to enjoy, how to relax. His sandy hair was tangled by the wind, and his hands looked as if they ached to do something. There was so much repressed energy in the man, she thought it quite possible he might explode from it.

Gillian could envision him galloping down a football field or even standing back, studying the opportunities in that quiet, reserved way of his, before exploding into action. In the past day, she had reassessed her original opinion of him. The first time she had met him, she dismissed him as a handsome but somewhat dull jock. Last night had proved her wrong. Though he took great pains to hide it, there was a certain passion and humor that he had, for some reason, tried to squelch. He couldn't keep either, however, from peeking out a little last night. It was downright intriguing, and she knew now why Leslie had liked him. They'd had more than a little in common, her partner and Steven: That barely visible fire that burned deep inside them, cloaked by a cool exterior. Break it open, and Gillian could only wonder what might emerge.

But could she do it?

And could she do it in time to help Sergei and his friends? As well as Steven and his development.

She stole another look at him. "I really enjoyed dinner last night," she ventured.

"So did I," he said with unexpected candor. "I don't often . . ."

He suddenly closed his mouth, and she wondered what he didn't often do. Surely not go out to dinner rarely. He wasn't her type at all, but he was successful and . . . attractive. He could have his choice of women. The thought suddenly hurt, which was totally ridiculous. Insane. Crazy.

But now as she drove up to the motel, she was only

too aware of his presence, of the electricity that sparked between them, of the sudden thick currents playing havoc with her senses. As she stopped and looked at him, she saw a similar confusion on his face that had ripped it of its usual mask. As if in sudden defense, he consulted his watch with an impatient gesture, and Gillian wondered if the intent was to intimidate her.

As he stepped out of the car, however, he stopped, obviously surprised by the sight in front of him.

To the side of the motel, in a grassy area, a man dressed in a cossack costume was guiding a spectacular white stallion in a circle as an attractive young brunette stood erect on the horse's back. As the rider saw Steven and Gillian, she executed a somersault, ending up on her hands on the cantering horse's back.

On another section of the motel's lawn, five acrobats were practicing, making human towers which would then collapse in a series of somersaults.

Color and activity were every place, and Gillian stole a look at her companion. As usual, he gave away little, but his gaze moved from activity to activity and then back to the white horse and rider, lingering there. A momentary streak of unexpected jealousy pierced Gillian, though she didn't understand why and tried instantly to banish it.

She didn't know, however, how successful that attempt would have been because Sergei, fully dressed in his ringmaster regalia, rushed up to her, followed by Alexei and his chimp, which gazed up at her adoringly. So did Alexei, much to her chagrin as she saw Steven's wry, questioning expression.

"Miss Gilly," Sergei said to Steven with his usual enthusiasm, "said you like maybe to see us, maybe to perform." His face was full of hope as he glanced at Steven. "Maybe to help us. We have best circus acts in Russia."

Gillian thought his face, so full of hope and optimism and goodwill, impossible to refuse. But Steven's face never changed, and she had the sinking feeling he resented being put on the spot like this, so she grabbed Sergei's arm. "Maybe," she said, somehow aware that Steven Morrow was relaxing slightly. "How did you get the horses today?"

Sergei turned toward the parking lot where a horse trailer stood. "Mr. Oaks, he bring them over. So many fine people. So many miracles." He turned back to Steven and beamed. "Miss Gilly, she . . . how do you say . . . liberty our animals back. She's *our* miracle."

"Liberate," Gillian corrected automatically and felt an unaccustomed flush flood her face as Steven gazed at her with those unfathomable gray eyes.

"Liberate?" he said. "Miss Gilly seems to have many talents. I'll have to hear more about that one."

Gillian couldn't quite tell from his tone of voice whether he was being sarcastic or not, but her attention was snatched from Steven by Romeo the chimp whose hand had reached for her.

"Another admirer, Miss Gilly?" Steven said, and

again Gillian couldn't quite catalog the tone. A tiny bit of amusement, perhaps. But what else?

"Do you like animals, Mr. Morrow?" she said, borrowing his sudden formality.

He shrugged, and again she couldn't read him. Without warning, she swung Romeo up, heavy as he was, into her arms and handed him to Steven, who had no choice but to take the chimp as the animal's arms went around his neck.

Gillian grinned at his discomfiture, as he stood there obviously at a loss of what to do. His eyebrows lifted as Romeo suddenly smacked him on the cheek with chimpanzee lips, and Gillian felt herself tense. Had she just ruined everything? Steven Morrow was one of the most unapproachable men she'd ever met, and now a monkey was . . . well, being rather . . . familiar.

She waited for a curt order, even departure, but instead he turned to her with a rueful look that was utterly mesmerizing. "Did you plan this, too, Miss Gilly?"

"That was Romeo's idea, I'm afraid."

"Romeo?" A dark eyebrow lifted.

A smattering of Russian filled the air as Alexei, apparently apologizing profusely, grabbed Romeo, obviously chastising him.

"It's all right," Steven said.

The chastising continued, and Romeo ducked his head in abject apology. Steven grinned, a charming open grin that completely stunned Gillian.

"Alexei doesn't understand English," Gillian explained.

"And you don't speak Russian? Or do you, among your many talents and miracles?"

Gillian grinned. She touched Alexei, made several gestures with her hands, then winked at Steven as Alexei grabbed her hand, kissed it, bowed to Steven and took Romeo in his arms and hurried off.

"Should I understand that?"

"A little pantomime. I'm learning it," she said. "You have to be part child to understand."

"And I don't qualify?"

"Do you, Mr. Morrow?" The challenge was open now, and more than the immediate question was being asked.

His gaze held hers for several seconds. "No," he said suddenly. "I don't suppose I do." He turned and walked away, but not toward the car as she feared.

He moved instead, a little like a cautious panther, through the grounds of the motel. There was a suspended trapeze apparatus, and he watched silently as several performers went through routines governed by space, and then on to jugglers. A mime, his face painted in black and white, came up and pantomimed a tragicomic routine. The motel grounds were a minicircus, held for the benefit of one, and Gillian held her breath as her companion said little while his eyes took in everything.

On the edge of the grounds, other bystanders stood, visitors attracted by the publicity and the plight of the circus. At times they clapped; at others merely looked on with curiosity. A television truck appeared, and men, loaded with camera equipment, approached Sergei.

Gillian looked at Steven and saw suspicion on his face, and she knew what he was thinking. That she was trying to trap him in some way. She was not going to lose by default.

She turned to Sergei. "We must go. I'll talk to you later." Without saying any more to Steven, she turned and headed for the car, trusting that he would not be far behind her.

Even though she had a long stride of her own, he beat her to her door and held it open for her. "I didn't plan that television crew," she said.

He studied her face for a moment. "It would have been a nice touch if you had."

"I didn't think of it," she said, bemused by his suddenly tolerant attitude.

His mouth crinkled up at the edge as if he were about to smile again, and then he retreated behind the enigmatic mask he usually wore.

As she stepped into the car, his hand touched her, and she felt a tingle go up and down her arm, and then her spine. She didn't move for a moment, not wanting to lose that contact or the sight of that slightly puzzled look which passed over his face. It made him look vulnerable for the first time since she'd met him. He'd always seemed so sure of himself.

His hand moved then, and she knew a sudden loss, as if something important had left her. She closed her eyes for a moment, trying to reestablish her equilibrium, to bring some sense into a situation that had no logic. She didn't even like Steven Morrow, even though he showed a bit more promise than she'd first thought.

She remembered why she didn't like him when his curt voice startled her to action. "I'm late."

Gillian wasn't sure how she, or he, for that matter, had gotten into the car. She was only aware now of his presence next to her, of the way the interior of the car was suddenly electrified.

She started the car, keeping her eyes off him, afraid that the confusion she was feeling would show in her face. She always wore her emotions openly, in her hand movements, in her walk. She had often envied Leslie's composure, the way she contained all her emotions under the serene expression. It was not until Connor MacLaren came along that her partner's eyes had softened and said what words could not.

Gillian drove swiftly and competently back to Steven's office, using the driving as an excuse for silence. She didn't know what to say right now, and that was most unusual for her. But she was still too full of that unexpected pregnant tension between them to spoil it.

He, too, was quiet although, as before, she sensed a tautness, a pressure in him that was identical to hers.

It was ludicrous. Yet exciting.

Gillian had never had this kind of reaction to a man before, had never felt anything like this silent but potent current that ran between them. It was only, she thought defensively, because they were adversaries.

There could certainly be no attraction. They had nothing in common. And he was a client. She had an unbreakable rule about involvement with a client.

So had Leslie, but she had broken hers.

But Gillian was positive *she* wouldn't. Especially with stubborn, inflexible Steven Morrow.

When they reached the office and the car came to a halt in the parking lot, Steven hesitated before getting out. His eyes were an even deeper gray, and Gillian had the strangest urge to put a finger near them and trace a line down to his mouth. Such an intractable face. Such a . . . memorable face. The slight scar on his face made it interesting. Or had it just become interesting in the past two days?

Now, as he looked thoughtful, the scar seem to deepen. "You were right about one thing," he said, and Gillian felt her heart jump. "They are great athletes."

Gillian looked at him with surprise. There was something in his voice, a kind of wonderment that made her think, for some reason, that he was startled by what he had seen. "You've never been to a circus before?"

"No." The answer did not invite any more questions but it raised all sorts of questions in Gillian's mind, that and a sympathy that made her ache. She had had a strange childhood of her own, but she'd seen circuses. Lots of them.

"Have you changed your mind then?" she said carefully.

"Perhaps on a limited basis." He looked at his

watch again, and unlocked his door and stepped out. He leaned over, and Gillian appreciated the athlete's body he still possessed, muscled yet lean. There was also an athlete's grace and surety when he moved. "Tell you what," he said. "Scale it down a little, and come back to me with a plan. I'll look at it."

Gillian felt herself smiling. "I'll have it for you."

"Include the horses."

Gillian felt her smile broaden. She thought she had detected a special interest in the horses. But she wasn't going to ask why. Not now. Not when everything was still so precarious.

"What time tomorrow?"

"Five," he said. "If that's not too late for you."

"Not at all."

"Thanks for the ride."

"Thanks for coming." Even Gillian heard the lilt in her voice, and she saw that slight twist of his lips which was nearly a smile, but not quite.

His hand lingered on the car door, just as his eyes lingered on her face. And then he nodded in response and turned, striding toward the building with that quick but easy stride of his. All of a sudden, she wished she had seen him play football, even if she'd never before had much interest in the sport. He would be spectacular running down the field. Darn, he was spectacular closing a car door.

Enough!

Gillian slammed the gear shift into reverse with unusual violence, felt the car shake with protest, and then heard the squeal of tires as she moved out of the parking place.

Why had he even halfway agreed to Gillian's suggestion?

Steven leaned back in his chair after his accountant, his last appointment of the day, left.

His accountant had recited the cold facts again. It was absolutely essential that the grand opening be a success. An increase in interest rates had severely depleted Steven's cushion. Not only did his builders need sales to survive and purchase more of his lots, but the country club operation itself must soon have more members to support it.

He had risked everything on this—on building a place where both adults and children could play and enjoy. A real community like he'd once dreamed about. But he was on quicksand, and the branch he held on to was flimsy. He needed sales, and he needed them quickly.

A circus. Did that convey the tone he wanted? In moderation, perhaps. Children would love it. Even he had been momentarily enchanted. Steven thought again of the white horses. He had dreamed of white horses as a boy, just as he had dreamed of a real home.

He had also dreamed of circuses, but circuses didn't come to small mill communities, and poor people without a car couldn't go farther to attend one. It was a dream he'd discarded and defensively labeled as unnecessary foolishness.

Fantasy had no place in the real world.

He thought over the plans for the opening. Gillian was right. There was little for the kids. Perhaps a circus act or two would be a drawing card. It certainly couldn't hurt. As long as it didn't interfere with the other activities.

With a slight smile he barely acknowledged, he leaned back in his chair and thought of white horses and dark brown eyes that twinkled just like the bangles of the costumes he'd seen that afternoon.

FOUR

Sergei's face was a study in agony. "But how to choose?"

Gillian shared his anguish. How *to* choose?

All the performers wanted to be included in the opening, but Gillian knew she couldn't push Steven Morrow too far.

"The Cossacks," she said. Steven had explicitly mentioned those.

"The Kuchouvos," Sergei said, mentioning the acrobats. "No equipment."

Gillian nodded.

"And Alexei?"

Gillian smiled. How could she exclude the exuberant Alexei? How could she exclude anyone?

They were all so good, all so eager. Performing was as important to them as food and drink. Sergei's face fell more and more as they had to make decisions.

The circus performers, she knew, were getting tired of pizza and even more weary of inactivity. They needed practice, and the limited space and facilities at the motel provided little of that. The sense of abandonment, of being marooned in a place where few of the performers spoke the language, was beginning to show.

Even Gillian's enthusiasm was cooled by the selection process. She had to find a way to use the entire circus. But how?

She kept imagining in her mind a community full of performers, resplendent in their costumes, holding sway over crowds of children. Why couldn't Steven Morrow see it?

Gillian returned to her office, and used the hated computer to put the program in proposal form, but she had difficulty concentrating. She kept remembering those enigmatic gray eyes, the way Steven Morrow had looked at the horses and the performers, the almost wry appreciation that he tried to hide. And she remembered the way her skin had tingled when he touched her, the singular excitement that had blazed between them. Even thinking about it made her shiver slightly.

But she wouldn't let it happen again. She wouldn't allow her body to betray her in such a preposterous way. She wouldn't. Business. That was all there was between them. All, her mind insisted.

As she left her own office and started for Steven's she ignored the now cloudy skies and lowered the top of her convertible. She desperately needed that sense of freedom to block out those troubling, inexplicable feelings.

But the internal excitement built as she pulled up outside Steven's office, as she walked through the door to the small outer office. Steven's secretary was on her way out. She was an older woman, dressed neatly in a business suit. Exactly what Gillian would have expected of Steven Morrow. They nodded cordially to each other, and then Gillian knocked on his office door.

She heard the spring of the step from inside the office and felt herself tense. She couldn't remember doing that before, not with a client.

As he opened the door, she noticed he was wearing his usual conservative clothes: A gray shirt that made his eyes look even darker, a pair of dark gray trousers, and a staid tie of striped shades of gray. Except for the absence of a suit coat, he looked as if he'd stepped out of *Gentleman's Quarterly*. Or at least what Gillian imagined emerged from a magazine with that image. She hadn't looked at it lately. She grinned at the thought. She'd never looked at it at all, except for letting her eyes roam over the cover as she did all magazines.

An eyebrow lifted inquisitively at her smile, and Steven Morrow suddenly looked anything but conservative. He looked, in fact, devilishly attractive.

Nonsense. Her idea of attractive was someone who looked comfortable in jeans and a sweatshirt, not a three-piece suit.

Nonetheless, she felt the rhythm of her heart jerk recklessly as her gaze found his and held it. Darn that serious, steady, determined expression that caught and pulled at something inside her.

"Miss Collins," he said politely.

"I thought we had gone beyond that."

"I know," he said, "but . . ."

But I want, need, to keep you at a distance. Although he never said the words, Gillian read the thought. She read it, because she felt exactly the same way.

"Mr. Morrow," she replied in the same level tone of voice.

He smiled then, the first really true smile she'd seen, and she thought, what a waste he didn't do it more often. The area around his eyes crinkled ever so slightly, and she found the smallest dimple in his left cheek. She longed to touch it. "Gillian," he finally said in a resigned voice, as if surrendering some important part of himself. "It's an unusual name."

"My mother didn't like ordinary names. I'm lucky. My sisters are Mirilla and Gianna."

His smile widened. "Are they all like you?"

"And what am I like?"

The smile disappeared, and the room seemed to darken. But his eyes were full of lively interest. "A little like a butterfly."

"Flighty?" she asked suspiciously, a little insulted.

His mouth twitched. "Difficult to pin down."

Gillian shook her head scoldingly. "Ouch . . . if that's a pun, Mr. Morrow."

"I don't have much practice."

"Now why do I believe that?"

"I really don't know, Miss Collins. You can come into my parlor and tell me."

Gillian was suddenly delighted with him. She had sensed a quiet, wry humor in him the other night . . . but whimsy? Never would she have guessed he'd have even an ounce of that in him.

But just as quickly as it had come, he obviously tried to banish that brief magic, although a vestige of it lingered in the room, like the echo of a bell. It couldn't be erased from the senses.

"Down to work, Gillian. What do you have for me?"

"Options A, B, and C." She handed him a blue binder.

"And which is your preference?"

Gillian hesitated. She had wanted to lead him to water, not force him to drink, which might alienate him completely. "Whichever you prefer," she said dutifully.

"Now why don't *I* believe *that*?"

Gillian wasn't sure she liked being this transparent. Again she revised her opinion of Steven Morrow. He was as quick as anyone she'd ever worked with. Quick and bright and perceptive.

And obviously not easy to manage.

"You never did tell me what happened to Leslie? Not an accident or illness, I hope."

The question caught her off guard. "Not unless you call love an illness," Gillian said before thinking.

He was sitting on the corner of his desk, dominating the room with his presence, but now he looked startled. "Leslie? In love?"

Damn. She and Leslie had agreed not to say anything until Leslie's plans were completed.

But that damned eyebrow was raised again, demanding that she continue. Gillian nodded, noting how odd it was that she was tongue-tied. She was never tongue-tied.

"May I ask with whom? Or for how long she'll be gone?"

He did have the right. Leslie had sold Steven Morrow's account and had serviced it. But Gillian inexplicably felt wounded. Was he so unhappy with her, then?

"She's in Chicago for a few days. I'm not sure when she'll be back."

"I'm glad she's all right," Steven said, stretching those long legs of his. "I was a bit worried about her. Leslie doesn't seem to be the type to . . . leave so suddenly."

"She wouldn't have," Gillian said defensively, "if I hadn't already worked on your account. She didn't think there would be a problem."

His eyes scrutinized her, and again Gillian felt as if he saw a lot more than she wanted him to see. "And you? Did you mind taking over?"

Gillian wished again he didn't appear to see so much. Why couldn't he be as dull as she'd first surmised?

"Of course not," she lied.

"Good," he said with a slight smile which said he

knew she lied. "Now let me take a look at your options A, B, and C." Gillian would have sworn she heard a teasing note in his voice, but his eyes were just as serious as they had been, and a smile no longer lurked on his lips.

She sat back, watching as he scanned her proposal. She couldn't read anything from his expression.

He walked around behind his desk and sat down, placing the binder on the surface of the desk. "And what do you recommend, Miss . . . Gillian?"

Gillian moved up on her seat, her hands gesturing as she spoke, as they always did. "I've been out to Cherokee Hills," she started carefully. "You have a lot of property, and the homes are spread out. You want people to visit as many of them as possible. If you have something going on in each neighborhood, they'll do that."

"So you want the third option?"

"I think it's the best, yes."

He leaned back in his chair, and Gillian couldn't tell what he was thinking.

"Let's drive out there," he said suddenly.

Gillian wasn't sure she was ready to spend more time with him in the close quarters of a car. It was too darn disconcerting.

"Or do you have something else you need to do?"

It was a challenge again, and as usual she responded to it. He appeared to have a total disregard for normal working hours, but then she did, too, since so many of her clients were in the entertainment field.

"All right," she said.

"You said you've been there?"

"Leslie took me there when we were first talking about the account."

"It's changed since then. A lot."

Gillian sensed the disapproval in his voice, and she didn't blame him. If everything hadn't moved so quickly, she would have been out there. If nothing else, she took pride in her work, in her thoroughness.

He shrugged. "It doesn't matter. I would rather show you myself, anyway." There was a distinct pride in his voice Gillian couldn't miss. Cherokee Hills was obviously much more than just a business to him.

They went in his truck again. He avoided the main thoroughfares, maneuvering in and out of rush-hour traffic like a race car driver as he spoke almost reverently about Cherokee Hills, one large planned community composed of several smaller neighborhoods, each grouped around a small park. It had been four years in the planning, and now, finally . . .

Gillian barely listened. She was too fascinated with the passion in his voice. Even she, who had scorned exactly this type of business, felt the seeds of excitement.

The entrance was bordered by brick walls and flower beds. The road divided just within, the island between lanes heavily wooded. It looked more like a park than another development until they reached a side road and swung right. A large sprawling stone complex seemed to meld into the woods to its right. On the left were tennis courts, and just beyond the courts a golf course.

She hadn't really looked at it before when she had driven out with Leslie. She hadn't thought she would have much to do with it, but now she noticed the care taken in preserving the land, to blend together the homes and the woods.

Somehow, this time it seemed natural to wait for him to come around to her door and to accept his hand, to even accept the fact that he held it a moment longer than necessary. Despite her best intentions, she also recognized the same warm, glowing tingle she'd felt earlier. Just as she was growing accustomed to it, Steven Morrow moved his hand, as if he himself had been burned. He led the way to the clubhouse, and everything was business again as he guided her through it, and then through two of the homes for sale.

When they had finished the tour, he drove her through the various communities, each built around its own little neighborhood park. It was, Gillian had to admit, more than "nice." Cherokee Hills was full of imagination and charm and character.

"Now you've seen it again, what do you suggest? Do you still suggest the third option?"

Gillian nodded. "It's perfect. You have the land, the space. The parks are made for this kind of thing."

"And the golf tournament? Won't a total circus take away from the focus of the opening?"

"Why does there have to be a focus? Something for everyone. Isn't that what you're trying to do here?"

Steven shook his head. "I've had several marketing

studies done," he said. "Leslie and I didn't decide on the golf tournament on whim."

His implication was only too clear, and Gillian felt her heart drop. And anger rise. She was damned good in her business, more instinctive than Leslie, who tended to go to the tried and true. And Cherokee Hills, despite Steven Morrow's repeated references to market studies and such nonsense, reflected a certain imagination of its own. It made her wonder exactly how much he really believed in them. "You can't measure heart or creativity," she said. "And Cherokee Hills has both of those."

There was a silence, and Gillian glanced at him for a reaction. But there didn't seem to be one.

"How did you get the animals back?"

Not understanding, she looked over at him with a question in her face.

"Your friend at the circus . . . he said you got the animals back. How?"

Did his mind always leap from one subject to another like this? She shrugged, a little embarrassed that the conversation had switched to her.

"How?" he insisted. "I'd read they'd been impounded, and then that they were returned. The paper didn't mention you."

Gillian was amazed, but then she had been that constantly since meeting him. He'd never even indicated before he was aware the circus was in town. She wondered whether he was really a sponge, soaking up everything and storing it in compartments just to surprise someone with a tidbit here and there when least expected.

"You knew about the circus?" she accused.

"I do read the papers, Miss Collins," he said, and she wondered if the tease was back in his voice or whether there was real indignation instead. She, who was so good at sensing moods and emotions in others, was completely at a loss with him.

"I didn't think you had time to read about frivolous things." Gillian didn't like the edge she heard in her own voice, but she was annoyed at the way he always threw her off balance.

"Tunnel-visioned, huh?" he asked, again with that amused challenge in his voice.

"*Are* you?"

"A little, perhaps," he said agreeably, "particularly about Cherokee Hills, but once in a while I try to stretch myself and read about circuses and such. And you didn't answer my question."

Gillian couldn't even remember the question now. What was there about this man that raised her hackles as well as something softer? It was, she supposed, that hint of self-mockery that occasionally crept into his voice, that said he really didn't take himself as seriously as sometimes his demeanor indicated.

Or was she just imagining it because she wanted to, because she didn't understand why her body was reacting to him, or even her emotions. It was downright scary.

"What question?"

"How you got the animals back?"

"Do you really want to know?"

They were stopped at a red light, and he looked over toward her. "Something tells me I should."

Gillian suddenly grinned, wanting to shake him as he had shaken her. "Blackmail," she said. "Pure and simple blackmail."

"What kind of blackmail?"

"I told the debtors who had filed to have the animals impounded that I would make Simon Legree and Scrooge look like Mother Teresa next to them if they didn't relent."

"And they believed you?"

Gillian knew she must look self-satisfied, but she had felt good about her trip to Boston and her rescue mission. "A few calls to the animal protection groups in the area, and we would have every one of them picketed. I just showed them it wasn't worth the trouble. They could never get the money from the circus; it just isn't there, and it isn't going to be there. So why make the animals suffer?" She suddenly beamed. "I made sure the newspapers knew about their sudden generosity in the name of international goodwill and animal well-being."

"And you? There was no mention of you."

"Of course not. A good public relations person is never in the paper. The clients get the credit, not the counselor. The whole concept would have been spoiled if anyone had suspected that the idea did not originate with the good people of Boston all on their own."

"Yet it would have been good publicity for your firm."

"I didn't do it for that."

"Why did you do it?"

Gillian shrugged, embarrassed. "The circus got a really rotten deal. It wasn't right, and someone had to do something." She grinned suddenly. "And after looking at some of those faces, how could you not do something?"

It wasn't *their* faces that worried Steven Morrow. It was *her* face. He was doing things now, thinking things, that he never would have envisioned weeks ago. Like asking her out to dinner again. He hadn't stopped thinking about that first dinner, how much he had enjoyed it, how much he liked that sparkle in her eye, and that sudden challenge in her voice, and the bouncing way she walked, as if nothing could hold her down.

For the first time in a very long while, he realized that he was lonely, deep down hungry for companionship. It scared him how much he enjoyed her company and how suddenly a room seemed empty when she left it.

The light changed, and he pressed his foot down on the gas, willing himself to forget those sudden thoughts. He didn't have time for romance. He couldn't afford it. He didn't know whether he could ever emotionally afford it.

His family's history had made involvement risky, and the one time he'd allowed himself to believe he could overcome that, he'd discovered certain unpleasant truths. Lorelie. Pretty Lorelie. She'd almost made him believe he could beat the odds. But when he'd lost his chance at the pros, he'd lost Lorelei. He had told himself at the time it was best, but the bitterness had lingered. Since then he had avoided anything but the most superficial relationships.

"Steven!"

His foot stomped down on the brake as he realized he had nearly run a red light. "I saw it," he lied with a grumble.

Gillian had to smile. Typical male response. But she held her tongue, watching his face. Confusion had flickered over it for a moment, before he reassumed direct control. She liked the confusion. She didn't like the control.

"Dinner?" he grumbled again. "It's late."

"You noticed," she replied cheerfully, looking at her own watch. Nearly nine. She glanced up at the sky, which was now a dark royal blue, illuminated by a gorgeous full moon.

He slid a sideways glance at her. "Is that sarcasm, Miss Collins?"

"Only a trace."

He grinned suddenly, and again she felt its impact. Dear God, it made her melt. She was beginning to be glad he didn't smile more or she would be reduced to a permanent pile of putty. "Is that a yes?"

"Not exactly. I have several dependents waiting for me at home. What about joining us for a macaroni casserole?"

"Dependents?" There was a definite question in his voice.

"No Name and Spenser. My cat and dog."

"Animals again."

"I seem to remember that you just shrugged when I asked you if you liked them? Do you?"

"Ummmmmmmm."

"I think you've invented a whole new language, specializing in noncommittal. I think I'll call it the Morrow language?"

"You don't give up, do you, Miss Collins?"

"Nope."

"And you won't let me retreat?"

"I didn't think athletes ever retreated. Or at least admitted they did."

"Strategic withdrawal has its advantages when planning a complicated play. Besides, I'm not an athlete any longer."

Gillian's eyes followed the lean muscular body from head to knees where his legs disappeared from view under the steering wheel. "No? I'll bet one month's retainer you run every morning." She allowed his first statement to go unchallenged though she wondered what complicated play he was contemplating.

"Would Leslie agree with that financial risk?"

"Probably not. She's the practical one. But she's not here. And you keep changing the subject. You don't really dislike animals?" She didn't think so, not the way he'd held the chimp or eyed the horses. But for some reason she wanted him to admit it, mainly because he obviously didn't want to.

She couldn't remember ever being so perverse. She'd sometimes teased clients, at times teased everyone, but she was usually more subtle than a Sherman tank about it.

"I don't suppose so," he finally admitted wryly, as if liking animals was a decided defect. "I've never been around them much."

"You didn't have a dog when you were a boy?" Her voice was horrified.

He hesitated, a muscle in his throat throbbing just the least little bit, and Gillian thought he was going to say something, but then he just shrugged. The Morrow language again. She wanted to sock him.

But in that slightest second, she also saw a vulnerability she hadn't seen before, a hurt pushed aside but not forgotten, and something inside her, in addition to the urge to sock him, wanted to take and hold him tight to her.

Just as she steeled herself for a refusal to dinner, he surprised her. "Is the offer for dinner still open?"

"Of course."

They arrived back at his parking lot, and she quickly gave him directions to her house in case he lost her while following her car. He didn't write anything down, just listened intently, and then nodded.

She started to leave the pickup, opening the door, and then hesitating.

"Second thoughts?" he asked, that eyebrow of his raised again.

"Lots of them," she admitted, but she knew her smile did nothing to rescind the invitation. "Don't you?"

They both knew exactly what she was saying, and it didn't concern dinner or business. The air was charged between them, like an electrical storm, and it wasn't likely to go static in the intimate setting of a home.

Yet as challenge ran from one to the other, neither could deny the magnetism that pulled them toward each other, that made it impossible to draw away.

His hand reached over and touched her cheek in a gentle, wondering gesture, a movement so expressive, so unlike the hard, indifferent shell he usually ducked behind, that she felt her heart crumble.

She lifted her head ever so slightly, just enough to invite a kiss. She felt her entire body strain toward him, felt the heat of his as he did the same.

And then his lips touched hers, lightly at first, exploring, but not for long. The bright, vivid attraction between them exploded, and his lips became as demanding as hers were seeking.

FIVE

Gillian had been kissed before. Many, many times, beginning in the sixth grade. She'd lived on a military base, and she'd always believed military brats learned about the birds and bees faster than anyone. She had, in fact, thought that she had experienced almost every type of kiss there was.

But nothing had prepared her for this!

She'd long ago discounted tales of fireworks. A myth invented by hopeless romantics. Although she'd shared some very nice kisses in the past, she'd never been rocked off her foundation.

Now she became a believer. Her toes tingled. Her heart pounded. Her breath came in gasps as the whole world tumbled like a juggler's ball. And then the lights in her head exploded, brilliant lights as his kiss deepened and his tongue seduced hers in a crazily sensuous courtship.

Gillian found herself responding as she'd never responded before, swept up in a need she'd never realized before. Her eyes flickered open and saw his, and for the first time she saw emotion in them, deep, raw feelings erupting in the usual calm grayness, making them glitter like silver reflected against the sun. Vibrant and alive.

She closed her eyes, relishing the feel of his mouth pressed against hers, the tangy smell of his after-shave, the slightly rough feel of his cheeks. She tasted the passion in him, yet she still sensed he was holding himself back, still maintaining an edge of control.

That didn't matter. Not at this moment. She only wanted to taste and feel and . . . care.

But she couldn't care.

Just as reality swooped into her mind, it must have also done the same for him, because he suddenly jerked away, as if burned. He looked at her, his expression puzzled, his eyes still glinting with something like excitement. Or passion. She watched as he tried to put it all in order again: The face, the mouth, the eyes. It was fascinating experience because he wasn't having a great deal of success.

"Damn," he exploded. "That was stupid."

He looked so consternated that Gillian, still rocked as she was by the power of his kiss, couldn't suppress a giggle. "It wasn't *that* stupid."

His eyes rested on her a moment, and then his lips twitched though he tried valiantly to stop them. "Do you ever take anything seriously?"

He looked at her warily.

"You do taste good," she ventured.

His lips twitched again. "So do you. Too good. I've never mixed business with pleasure before."

"Me either."

"It's not a good time to start," he said, though his eyes still seemed to glint.

"Nope," she agreed.

"But I *am* hungry."

"Good."

"For food," he qualified, seeing the glint in *her* eye.

"Of course."

But neither of them moved. Gillian felt she'd just been turned into a pillar of salt, so rooted to the seat she was. She tried to remember which particular biblical figure also had that problem, but her mind wasn't working in its usual patterns. In fact, it wasn't working at all. Damn, she was paralyzed.

Using all her will, which was minimal at the moment, she tried a finger. It moved. Slowly, the rest of her did the same as she slid from the truck. Her mind registered only the slightest surprise that he hadn't tried to help her this time. Could he be suffering the same paralysis?

She stumbled more than walked to her car, trying desperately to regain her composure. She was still feeling his lips on her, still registering the surprise that he'd agreed to come, still overcoming her astonishment that she'd asked him.

The world was moving in a most topsy-turvy way.

Had Leslie felt the same, been caught in a momentum that allowed no thought or caution or even plain good sense?

She climbed into her car. The top was still down, and most of her friends would have been horrified at her carelessness. But Gillian had always felt that a thief, if he wanted the car badly enough, would find a way in, and probably ruin the locks doing so. She'd also hoped that a thief would think no one would be stupid enough to leave a car unprotected and believe it must be some kind of trap.

At any rate, even the Princess, as she'd termed her car, was the last thing on her mind now. Why had she invited him? He would probably be horrified at her apartment. No that she cared. Not that she cared at all.

Christ. Not only had she not locked her car, she had left the top down. He'd never met anyone quite so . . .

He hunted for a word, but couldn't quite find one as he pulled out behind her. He'd started with irresponsible, but in the past few days he'd discovered she wasn't that. She did her homework, and the ad she'd created was damn good. Her ideas weren't bad either. Perhaps not exactly what he'd had in mind, but they had some merit. He just wasn't quite sure whether he was ready to change his whole concept or not.

Steven knew he was rigid about some things. He'd had to be. Long ago, he learned that to achieve anything he had to set goals and stick with them, to cast aside distractions and avoid detours. There were no shortcuts. Every time he'd tried to take one, he'd faced disaster. He also realized he was driven to succeed and knew it was rooted in the past. Poverty was so damned scarring, and he felt covered with scar tissue.

The little red sports car made a turn, and he almost missed it. The car was like her; it spurted ahead with bouncy energy, and he suddenly felt heavy and weighted in the practical pickup. If not irresponsible, what was the word he searched for? Fresh. Irreverent. Spontaneous. Like a bubble. A bubble in the air. He'd grabbed for one once when he was a child, when another boy made bubbles from a little glass jar by blowing through a wire holder. It had disappeared at his touch, but it was so beautiful for those few seconds, the colors magically iridescent.

And what did he want with a bubble? Something so fragile.

For the life of him, he didn't know why he was doing this, why he was following her home, why he had said yes. Why he had kissed her.

For a moment he'd felt warm and contented . . . and human for the first time in a very long while. At dinner the other night, during their verbal fencing in his office and returning from the circus the other day and then, again, tonight. Suddenly, he realized how much of a machine he'd become in the past few years. He'd had satisfaction, of course, and even pleasure when a development turned out well and profitably.

But warmth? No, and it was a feeling he didn't want to let go.

Damn Miss Gillian Collins.

As Gillian drove into the long driveway of the seventy-year-old home that sat majestically on a hill, she noted in her rearview mirror that Steven Morrow was sticking with her like glue. She should have known.

She hoped he didn't assume she lived in the stately home, or he would be bitterly disappointed. Why did she care what he thought? She suddenly resented him because she did just that. And she didn't like it one bit.

She drove around to the back, to the small cottage that had once been a garage, and she saw Spenser sitting in the window. He often edged his fat sausage body up on the sofa ledge where he could look out for her, or just perhaps look out at the world.

She parked and watched as Steven drove the pickup truck next to the Princess. Beauty and beast, she thought suddenly, whimsically, and felt better. She knew she had a grin on her face when he met her on the doorstep.

That attractive eyebrow rose again, and she looked suggestively at the two vehicles standing side by side. He smiled wryly. "The odd couple," he offered.

Gillian laughed, and her nervousness left her. He did have an unexpected sense of humor that was utterly enchanting. "Something like that," she said. "And beware, you may be attacked by anxious beasts when we go in."

She opened the door, and he noticed she hadn't bothered to lock the cottage. He started to say something and then she turned, and he knew she expected him to. He swallowed his words. He refused to be predictable—at least this once.

There was a bark, a sort of muffled greeting, and Steven winced as he saw the dachshund waddling toward them, the whole body wriggling with something close to ecstasy. Behind the walking sausage strolled, quite regally, the ugliest cat he had ever seen in his entire life.

"Your protection, I presume," he said in a droll tone.

Her dark eyes sparkled in a way that made his heart warm again. "Well Spenser anyway. He might lick an intruder to death." She leaned down, and her finger nuzzled the dog's ears to the accompaniment of a happy growling sound. "This is Spenser, after the detective, of course. The long nose, you see. And No Name, who prefers not to be categorized by a name."

"She told you this, of course," he said with grave interest.

Gillian looked insulted. "You *haven't* been around animals much. She's a he."

Steven suddenly felt the need to defend himself. "Well, Spenser's obvious."

Gillian grinned. He'd suddenly looked like a chagrined lad at being caught on such an error. "Well, not exactly. Spenser is an 'it.' Of course, so is No Name, but they don't know it, so watch your leg." She knew she was running on, many of her words utterly nonsensical and hard to follow. But he seemed to be managing.

Now he looked fairly nonplussed, so unlike his usual confident self, that Gillian had to smile. "Don't worry," she said. "I'll warn them to cease and desist. If you behave, that is."

"And what does 'behave' entail?" he said, uncertain of the ground rules.

"You have to like my cooking," she said.

"At this moment, I think I would like anything edible."

She tipped her head and regarded him solemnly. "Do I hear a note of skepticism in your voice?"

"Only raw hunger," he replied with a half grin. "Of the carnivorous kind."

Gillian raised one of her eyebrows now, in a gesture much like his own. "Predatory, huh?"

He eyed her speculatively. "Yep."

She grinned. "Then I'd better feed you before you start stalking Spenser. A drink?"

"The dog was not what I had in mind."

"I know," she replied with a grin, ridiculously pleased that the lustful glint was back in his eyes. "And about that drink?"

"What do you have?"

"Beer. Wine. And gin and tonic."

"A beer, thanks."

Again, she raised her eyebrow questioningly, and he realized she hadn't expected his answer. He wondered why.

But she was turning away. "I'll be right back. Can

you let Spenser out?" She didn't wait for an answer, but disappeared through a door.

Steven felt at a complete loss. How in the hell do you let a dog out? On a leash? Without a leash? Just as he pondered the question, his gaze searching for some kind of lead, her voice drifted through the doorway. "You can't chase him away with a stick. Just open the door."

He did as he was told, feeling a bit like an alien on a strange planet. And then he looked around the room. He hadn't known exactly what to expect, but he found he wasn't surprised at what was here. There was an old sofa, plump and comfortable looking, that sat in front of the window; a few similarly cozy-looking chairs, including a huge beanbag chair sitting in the middle. There were plants everywhere, and some pale green curtains were pulled back to allow the sun entrance. Probably the newest thing in the room was a sound system. He recognized the quality of its components, and his eyes gazed over the collection of recordings: Some old records, some compact discs, some cassettes. It was an eclectic mix, ranging from jazz and classical to folk music, from music of the fifties and finally to today's soft rock.

"I like everything," said a soft, amused voice, and he whirled around. She was standing in the doorway, a beer in one hand, a glass of wine in the other. "What do you like?"

He shrugged. "A little of everything, too, I suppose."

"A definitive answer, please," she said.

"Okay. Hank Williams." For some reason, he thought that might throw her, if only a small bit.

She grinned, thrust a beer into his hand, and went to one of the shelves of a bookcase next to the sound system, and triumphantly emerged with a record. "One of my favorites," she said a little smugly as she put it on, and the haunting words of lost love, as only Hank Williams could sing them, filled the room. Steven wished he hadn't been so clever. He didn't think he wanted to hear about lost love at the moment, nor the wistful longing of the whiskey-voiced Williams.

She was altogether too close, her mouth too inviting as she looked up at him. The room suddenly became very compressed, the air very alive with static energy.

He looked down. She was always so full of life, that he lost his awareness of her small size. She was not short, but neither was she very tall, and now that she'd taken off her heels, the top of her head came to below his chin. She was looking up at him, her head tipped in that delightfully impish way that made his heart respond in an odd rhythm. Her eyes were sparkling with mischief, though there was a bit of chagrin in them as if she'd lost a fight of her own, and he found himself leaning down.

His lips touched hers and felt her response. His arms went around her, bringing her closer.

An impatient bark sounded, and then another, and

she backed away slightly. "His Lordship," she mumbled although her gaze didn't waver from his face.

Another bark came. Then a meow from inside.

"Do they always conspire together?"

"Just until they're sure of the visitor."

"How long does that take?"

Her laugh rippled down his spine. "No one's ever stayed long enough to find out."

"Easily intimidated?"

"Doesn't say much about me, does it?" she said.

"Doesn't say much about your visitors."

The bark grew louder, the meow more plaintive. "You haven't had the full treatment yet."

"Another challenge?"

Gillian looked at him. He had rolled up his shirtsleeves and loosened his tie. His hair was mussed, as if he'd run impatient fingers through it, and he looked terribly appealing as those deep gray eyes regarded her so seriously. Despite the light banter, however, his mouth was unsmiling. She swallowed, thinking how much she wanted to see that trace of a dimple again, the trace that came only with his rare smile.

"Are you up to it?" she finally replied.

His hand went out and touched her cheek. Softly, even gently, and it surprised her so much, she stepped back. His hand instantly fell to his side. "I'm not sure," he said in that grave voice that shook her down to her toes.

She knew she was gazing shamelessly up at him, but she didn't seem able to stop. Nor, apparently, did he notice, because he was staring at her with the same obvious intensity.

The vocal level of the barking increased and finally jarred Gillian to action. "I'd better get Spenser," she whispered.

"Uh-huh," he agreed in a low tone that sounded like a soft rumble.

When she opened the door, Spenser came wriggling in, demanding attention, and the momentary spell was broken.

"I'll see to dinner if you'll see to Spenser's emotional well-being by scratching his ears."

"Is that the prescription for emotional well-being around here?" he asked, a gleam in his eyes.

Gillian laughed. He kept surprising her with that offbeat humor of his, always when she least expected it.

"One of them," she agreed, and then ducked through the doorway to the kitchen before her feet became fixed to the ground again and she totally humiliated herself.

She had salad makings, and the casserole she'd prepared last night for use this weekend. It was one of her favorites—macaroni and cheese and tomatoes and hamburger, all spiced very liberally—but it was simple fare indeed. She'd already put it in the oven, and now she checked it and started making the salad when his head appeared in the doorway.

"Mission accomplished. An emotionally satisfied dog is now snoozing on your sofa. May I help?"

"Do your talents extend to slicing tomatoes."

"And beyond. I can even pull lettuce on occasion. And what do I smell?" He sniffed appreciatively.

"I hope you like spices."

"I'm learning to like spice very much." The implication was clear as he looked toward her. His mouth twisted in a smile, a real smile though not a wide one. The dimple peeked out. The knife fell from Gillian's hand, and she had to hop to keep it from slicing off a part of her foot. Her arm hit the bowl of lettuce and it went scattering over the kitchen floor, the bowl making a thud, and she lost her balance and went down on the floor, her glass of wine following. A bark came from the other room, and a thud, and then Spenser was wandering through the lettuce as No Name sniffed it disdainfully.

"So much for salad," Gillian said ruefully to disguise the flush she knew was spreading across her face. She was usually not clumsy. Now she felt like the greatest klutz in the world. How could he do that to her? Just his presence made her all thumbs.

She looked up at him. He was grinning. It was the first real grin she had seen on his face. And he was actually chuckling.

Gillian couldn't decide whether to be entranced or insulted. She opted for entranced. How could she ever have though him dull or stuffy? The area around his eyes was crinkling, the dimple had emerged in full force, and he looked years younger. He leaned down and offered her his hand and easily pulled her up. He didn't let go, however, but held her close to him, the grin slowly disappearing. "You aren't hurt?"

"Only my pride."

"It shouldn't be. You looked delectable there among the lettuce."

"You *are* hungry."

"Apparently not as much as Spenser," he said, looking down, and her eyes followed his. The dog was gobbling up wine-soaked lettuce.

"He eats anything," she explained, still holding his hand. It was so warm. Warm and strong and compelling. She tried to keep her voice light, to keep from looking at him. "No need for a garbage disposal here."

The grin was gone from his face now, and it was intense again, as it so often was. She suddenly realized she *liked* that intensity, now that she was getting used to it. Dear God, getting used to *him*. Heaven help her.

She looked down at the hand he was holding, and suddenly it was free, as if he, too, just realized he was still clasping it.

His voice, teasing just a moment ago, was cool courtesy again as he offered to help clean up. "Towels? Napkins?"

Gillian's mind went blank. Towels. She'd meant to get some today, along with napkins. And coffee. And . . .

Gillian bit her lip. She'd never been real good at niceties, but now she felt totally embarrassed. Steven Morrow confused her as she'd never been confused before, befuddled her in a way she'd thought impossible, reduced her to . . .

The heck he would, she thought suddenly, her spirit bounding back.

She looked up at him again, and he was smiling, as if fascinated as he studied her, the silver in his eyes gleaming. Her chin went up, and he stepped closer. "I love watching you think," he said, that slightest tease in his voice.

"You must not have much excitement in your life," she retorted, again not sure whether she should be insulted or not.

"That's being remedied," he said, arching that eyebrow of his.

Gillian had to smile. "I guess it is," she agreed. "But if you ever want anything to eat, you'd better leave my kitchen."

"An order?"

"A suggestion to the hungry."

But when he left, obviously reluctantly, the room suddenly felt empty, the life drained from it. She found an old dish towel in a bottom drawer and made a halfhearted attempt at wiping the floor, then checked the casserole. The cheese was bubbling away. As the only thing left edible in the house, she didn't want to destroy that too.

She set the table, hoping he wouldn't notice the lack of napkins, and stood there looking at it for a moment. It was ungodly plain. She poured the rest of the wine from the bottle she'd opened into a pitcher, then stuck a candle in the bottle and lit it. The light flickered, casting a romantic glow over the kitchen.

She almost pinched it out again. The last thing she needed now was romantic. Yet she couldn't bring herself to do it. She thought of his grave face lit by candlelight, and she felt herself smiling.

Dammit.

SIX

Steven found himself prowling the cottage like a restless beast.

His self-control, so painfully constructed over the years, was falling to pieces around him. He wanted Gillian. He wanted her so badly, he hurt. And she wasn't even his type, he mused disgustedly. In the past few years, what little romancing, escorting, he had done had been with smooth, sophisticated women.

They had, in fact, been like Lorelei, and in a flash of self-examination he wondered whether he had leaned that way in some kind of self-defense, that he knew he wouldn't trust a woman like that, not really, and so they were safe. He wouldn't become emotionally involved. And thus he wouldn't be hurt.

Christ, he remembered that day in the hospital when Lorelei had returned his engagement ring, the one he'd saved for months to buy her. The doctors had told him he would never play football again, that he would, in fact, probably have trouble with that leg

throughout his life. And he'd told her. She had been
silent, then she left. Three days later she'd returned
his ring. No more football hero. No more pro athlete
prospects. No more Lorelei. Even now, he felt the
bitterness of that betrayal, but not regret. How could
he regret losing something he'd never really known?
But it had taken him months to realize he had indeed
never known her. Or even himself for that matter. She
had been like icing on a cake, and he'd been very
hungry for cake. He'd been like a greedy boy then,
suddenly faced with a banquet after starving, and he
hadn't known how to choose and when to quit.

He prided himself on learning, though, of taking
things with moderation. But he felt no moderation
with Gillian Collins and thus she was a danger to him.

But he couldn't help but grin as he remembered
her sitting among the lettuce with such a surprised
look on her face, and then the succeeding emotions.
There had been a little bit of everything, each alive
and vibrant.

He had never met anyone quite as spontaneous
and open. Gillian Collins, he knew, had probably
never done anything halfway. She didn't know how to.

Steven felt something rub itself against his leg, and
he looked down at Spenser. He was a ridiculous-look-
ing animal with his long nose and floppy ears and
distorted body, but he now looked up at Steven with
something close to adoration, and Steven found himself kneeling and rubbing ears again. He wasn't quite
sure whether he liked the resultant swipe of a tongue
on his face. "We'll make a bargain, you and I," he said.

"I'll rub your ears if you promise not to bark at inopportune times."

Spenser gave him a suspicious, albeit I'll-do-anything-for-a-rub look, and Steven wondered what in the heck he was doing. Making deals with a dog was not rational behavior. But then he hadn't been rational since Gillian walked into his office.

He sipped his beer and looked around again. There was a comforting warmth about the cottage. There were numerous photographs, and he rose and walked over to them. He recognized Gillian with two other girls, all three of them bearing an uncanny likeness. There was a man in the uniform of a staff sergeant, and a slender woman with long black hair. There were photos of animals and one of her and Leslie together. In all of them, Steven could almost sense the vitality and energy of Gillian Collins, a kind of glow that said "I love life and dare you to do the same."

He thought of his own home, a condominium bare of all but necessities. He didn't even have pictures of his two brothers, one married and with children in California, and the other still a bachelor here in Atlanta.

"Steven."

He turned around, his hands still on the picture he'd picked up to get a closer look. "Your parents?"

"Yep. My mother is part Indian, part Mexican, and wholly gypsy at heart. My dad's Scotch and Scandinavian. It's a weird combination."

"Where are they?"

"Germany. With the Army."

"And your sisters?" He tried to remember their names but only recalled how unusual they were.

"Left in various places around the world." She grinned. "Mirilla married an Italian when Dad was stationed in Italy, and Gianna married an Air Force pilot, who's now training pilots in Saudi Arabia. I was sorta left here when Dad was stationed at Fort McPherson. I'd just started college at the University of Georgia and decided to stay. For a while."

"For a while?"

"I think I've become accustomed to wandering," she said. "I always think maybe tomorrow."

"And your business?"

"I suppose that's what holds me here now—that and Leslie—but now that . . ." The words dangled off.

"Now that?" he prompted.

Gillian shrugged. "I came to tell you dinner's ready," she said, avoiding the question. She really didn't want to think about Leslie now, and what her absence would mean. Leslie had been her best friend as well as her partner, even her anchor.

It seemed natural to Steven to put his arm around her shoulder as they walked into the kitchen. The aromas were even more enticing now, and he felt a rumbling in his stomach. He was used to going long periods of time without eating when engrossed in a project. He had a way of concentrating that kept everything out except the immediate problem, something he had learned playing football when he had to block the noise of the crowd, the taunts of opposing players, the threat of a tackle when he was ready to throw. He had honed that ability to a fine art, and sometimes found he had gone a day without food.

Candlelight flickered, and he was inordinately pleased that she had added that special touch. As she sat down, he noticed that the light seemed to make her dark hair glow with a special sheen, and her eyes appeared even brighter than usual.

She was really quite beautiful, and she seemed to grow even more so every moment he spent with her. That, certainly, had never happened to him before.

Gillian grinned at him. "Eat," she commanded, and he obeyed, finding to his surprise that the casserole was really quite good. Wonderful, in fact. She had sliced some tomatoes to go with it, and there were some biscuits. He ate. And ate. And ate until he looked up and saw her looking at him with appreciative amusement. "You *were* hungry," she commented.

"Your fault," he said, strangely disconcerted at realizing he had attacked the meal as he usually attacked a problem, disregarding even the barest civilities. "It's great."

"Not everyone's as impressed," she said. "Leslie always runs for a glass of ice water after eating my cooking. Too much hot pepper. Even Spenser pauses a moment."

Steven looked down at the dachshund which was looking up at him with expectant eyes, and then Steven's eyes fell to his own cleaned plate. "Sorry, fellow," he said.

"He just wants you to think I starve him to death."

"No one would make that assumption," he said, the skin around his eyes crinkling up with amusement. "More macaroni?"

"You want me to look like Spenser," he accused.

"Now that *would* be interesting." She tipped her head as if imagining such a sight. "Let's see, we can get a nose job, but those ears just won't do at all." She shook her head sadly. "Won't work. Sorry."

He looked at her soulfully. "Another rejection."

"Ha, now I don't believe that. The great football hero."

Gillian had been teasing him, but now she saw him tense, the momentary relaxation gone as if it had never been there. She had hit a nerve, but she wasn't quite sure what it was.

"Steven?" she said, her voice questioning.

But he was shoving his chair back. "I'll help you clean up." His voice was curt, businesslike again.

Miserably, Gillian rose with him. She didn't protest, mainly because she didn't think it would do any good. She'd witnessed that stubbornness of his more than once. But even more than that, she didn't want him to leave the room. Although he had suddenly, visibly, and unquestionably walled her out, she still didn't want to lose his presence, even if it made no sense.

He stacked and rinsed the dishes with the easy, almost professional efficiency of one who had done it often. It was work without conversation, other than a brief question about a possible dishwasher—there was none—and the whereabouts of soap—under the counter. It was almost like having a stranger, even a genie, taking over her kitchen. She could only stand there uselessly and watch. She didn't dare try to assume control, and that wasn't like her at all.

She watched him, the quick, sure movement of his hands, the tenseness in his shoulders, the serious look back on his face, the eyes that no longer held that teasing light but were altogether too grave.

What had she said that had taken away that lightness that she'd so liked?

He knew a lot about her now. She realized she had chattered a quite deal about herself, but she also realized he had said nothing about himself. He was as much a mystery today as when she'd first walked into his office days ago. More so, in fact, for he'd offered just enough puzzle pieces to fascinate her. She was greedy for more, so she could fit the whole thing together. She went over what she had.

A real estate mogul who seemed very at home in her small kitchen eating macaroni.

A macho jock who took over her kitchen as if it were the most natural thing in the world.

An austere man who hated to admit to emotions, yet had obviously captured Spenser's heart if the dog's adoring look was any measure.

A three-piece suit who'd seen momentary magic at the sight of the white circus horses.

He was one contradiction after another, intriguing and challenging.

But now he was finishing the dishes, then attacking

the sink and the counters as if they were an enemy.
When he finished they looked more pristine than anytime she'd cleaned them.

Steven hesitated after taking one last swipe, then
turned to her. "Thank you for dinner."

"Are you Mr. Clean in disguise?" Gillian found
herself asking, still amazed at the sequence of events.

His mouth relaxed slightly. "Not exactly. Habit, I
suppose. I was the oldest of four boys, and my
mother . . ." His eyes clouded, and he didn't finish.
Something like pain flickered across that usual emo-
tionless face, and Gillian wondered why it was so difficult for him to talk about his own family.

But whatever he was going to say, he eventually
thought better of it. "I think it's time to go. I still have
work to do tonight."

"Steven . . . ?"

His steady gray gaze met hers, waiting for her to
continue.

And she couldn't. She wanted to ask him to stay.
She wanted to ask him so many things. But his expression was closed, as if he'd made up his mind about
something and wouldn't change it. Gillian thought
then she had never met anyone quite so disciplined
before. At one time, she would have said rigid, but not
now. Disciplined was the correct word.

And yet she had seen it drop just a little tonight,
had seen a chink in that heavy armor he wore. "We'll
talk tomorrow," she said finally. "About the opening."

"The opening," he emphasized. "And thanks
again for the meal." Just then he looked down, and

Gillian followed his gaze. Spenser was twisting his elongated body around him with unabashed longing. He leaned down quickly and gave the dog a swift pat as it wriggled even more enthusiastically.

Steven shook his head with a certain rueful air. "He's shameless."

So was she, Gillian thought, as her breath caught in her throat. He looked magnificent in her small room, his tall, fit body dominating it, and the light catching a glint of gold in his sandy hair. He filled the room with quiet, unassuming but compelling magnetism, and she knew he was completely unaware of it. Her hand curled up in a fist as she fought against reaching out with it to touch him.

"When?" she said.

"Call my secretary in the morning," he said almost curtly, as if the words were jerked from him. He didn't move though, and she felt frustration emanating from him, as though he detested his own weakness in not wanting to leave. Frustration and even a kind of self-directed anger.

And then she was leaning toward him, her face reaching upward and his moving downward until their lips met.

It was a soft, searching meeting, an inevitable kind of kiss that carried a sense of wonder about it. But the tenseness was still in his body, and she knew he was fighting against the attraction that was so electric between them. Yet his lips were gentle as they explored and tested. His mouth opened, and his tongue darted along her lips, inviting her lips to part, and they did, so very naturally.

As just hours before, Gillian felt herself catch on fire, a case of spontaneous combustion that closed out anything else: caution, common sense, responsibility. It was as it had been earlier in this same room, as if they had never been interrupted by Spenser and No Name. The only thing of importance was the feel of his lips against hers, the awakening sensations teased by his tongue, the warmth of his body as it pressed against her.

Gillian wanted as she had never wanted before, and the uniqueness of that want, the power of that want, made her tremble. She craved an intimacy with this man, one she'd never wanted with another. But she knew she was risking a great deal, nothing less than her heart.

And she wasn't sure he would treat it kindly.

His lips had left her mouth now, and were moving across her cheek to her ear. He pushed her hair back, and he maneuvered around a hoop earring to nibble on the lobe of her ear. She felt tiny little explosions detonating everyplace, and her hands went around his neck, her fingers playing with the crisp sandy hair.

She felt his manhood harden against her, and waves of delectable anticipation ran through her as she responded by snuggling into the curve of his body.

"Ah Gillian," he whispered in her ear. "This isn't wise."

Gillian gazed up at him, wishing she knew him better, wishing she knew what he was thinking. But he was still keeping that to himself. "You said that before," she said.

"I know. I'm not doing a very good job of following my instincts."

"Or maybe you are," she whispered.

He pulled her closer, hugging her tightly to him, as if afraid to let her go, and it was as revealing an action as she'd seen from him. "Damn," he said. "You feel so . . . huggable."

"Good," she said.

"Not good. Why can't you feel like a lump of coal?"

That was a question without an answer, and Gillian could give him only a wobbly grin. After his reaction tonight at dinner, she didn't know which words were safe and which weren't.

But he didn't give her time to think anymore. "I really do have to go, Miss Collins," he said softly, letting his voice caress the last word for a moment, even as she realized he was trying to distance himself again. He didn't allow himself any more time to react. He stepped away and moved toward the door. "Good night," he said and was gone before she could even answer him.

Gillian slumped against the wall, full of emotions that had no place in her life, even as she realized she still knew absolutely nothing about the man who was turning her world upside down.

❖────────❖

Damn, but he had acted the idiot several times today, Steven thought as he drove away. Why couldn't he keep his libido under control around her?

The problem was, it wasn't only his libido that was kicking up. Too many other emotions were also involved, and they were the dangerous ones, so dangerous. He couldn't ever remember melting at the sight of a smile before, even Lorelei's.

But that particular smile, the wistful, forlorn smile when he'd so rudely asked her to call his secretary, didn't belong in a face that usually glowed with vitality and inner joy. It had filled him with regret, even shame, and he'd wanted to erase it. And then that chemistry betwen them kicked in again.

He knew he should get another agency. This . . . business relationship . . . wasn't working. He needed to keep his wits about him. Too much depended on the next few weeks for him to be blindsided by a woman.

But it was too late now. Too much work was already in her hands.

Why had he permitted that last kiss? He'd almost been able to force himself away, especially after she had said something about the "great football hero." Steven hated that image, and part of Gillian's attraction for him had been her obvious indifference to the fact. And then she'd referred to it, and he had gone cold all over again. He'd been able to stiffen his resolve. Until she had looked at him . . .

Blinders. He needed blinders when she was

around. If he couldn't do it physically, by God, he would do it emotionally.

Somehow.

But how he ached now! A shower, that's what he needed. A cold shower. A very, very cold shower.

Fogged, tired, and completely out of sorts, Gillian found herself at the Atlanta newspapers the next day. She did have other clients, after all, and she knew she had neglected that fact during the past few days.

She was also a bit angry. At herself. At him. He had no right to do this, to turn hot and cold like a shower head gone berserk.

She gave a news release on a new nightclub opening to the entertainment editor, joked a few minutes, turned down an offer of lunch, and then started to leave when she had a sudden thought.

"Do you think I can use the morgue?" she said, referring to the newspaper library.

"Sure, if I go up with you," the editor, a longtime friend with whom she'd hoisted a few beers, said. "What do you want to know?"

She shrugged. "I'm sort of filling in for my partner. We have a client . . . Steven Morrow."

"The quarterback," the man said smugly. "One of the best Georgia's ever had."

"Not you too," she sighed. "I would have thought better."

"Hey, I went to Georgia then," Hal said.

"Godalmighty, but he could throw a football. Run too."

"What happened?"

He shook his head at her dismal ignorance. "An accident . . . bad tackle near the end of the season. Took him out of the running for the Heisman. Took him out of football altogether. We started losing."

Gillian had the terrible feeling that he felt worse about losing than Steven's injury, and she wondered whether that was the common reaction. Perhaps that was why Steven was so sensitive about it. After running over their conversation all night, she could only surmise that her seemingly innocent comment about football had started his retreat.

She went up to the morgue with the reporter, and together they found the file of clippings about Steven Morrow. When he left her for lunch, she sorted through the photographs, sports stories, and profiles. She was hungry for any knowledge, even the slightest hint of what made Steven Morrow tick. But it was obvious, even then, he valued his privacy. In one story, it mentioned a family in a north Georgia community, but said little else of a personal nature. Most of the clippings were glowing accounts of his accomplishments on the football field, and then a bunch of stories right after the injury. There was one of him being carried off the field, his face a portrait of pain.

Then there were several later ones, a brief announcement of his appointment as vice president for a development firm, and several more brief stories about his private developments, and then a large one, prepared, she knew, by Leslie, about Cherokee Hills.

She looked at her watch. She'd been here two hours, and she had a desk full of work. She'd learned little more than she already knew, except for the injury. She thought back. Though most of the time, he moved with a purposeful grace, she had noticed late in the day that sometimes he slowed, and even once had limped. She had accounted it to a twist of an ankle or something similar.

Gillian shook her head. No more time to wonder. She had told him she would call, but had postponed it all day. She wasn't sure she was up to talking to him, or even his secretary. But now she had to. She had to know what he'd decided about the circus and the grand opening.

Sergei was counting on her. She was counting on herself. She had never been a quitter, and she didn't plan to start now. She thought of herself a week ago, and how she had been amused at her partner's odd behavior once she'd fallen in love.

But no one, absolutely no one, she decided, was acting more strangely than she at the moment.

It had to stop.

A client, she told herself. Just a client. A very difficult client.

He was nothing more.

Absolutely not!

SEVEN

Steven Morrow gazed over Cherokee Hills from the bluff on which the clubhouse sat. Since the first shovel of earth turned on the development, he'd taken pleasure in doing just this. Watching the creation of something he'd planned.

But today, for some reason, it didn't give him the usual pleasure. For the first time in years, he felt that something important was missing from his life, something vital and life-giving.

He didn't want to analyze it. Not now. He knew deep down he was afraid to. He didn't want to lose control of his life. And he knew that what was nagging at him might do just that. It already had, to a certain extent.

Last night was a disaster. How could he have allowed himself to do that? Kiss her. Not only once but three times, each leading deeper into a quagmire of trouble. A business associate! The top no-no on a sacred list.

Discipline, he warned himself. Discipline. He had learned discipline at an early age, when he was ten and his father was injured and started drinking more than ever. He had to take over a lot of responsibility for his siblings. Why had it deserted him now?

He thought of his brothers, Mike and Bobby, and tried to remember the last time he had seen them. They both tried to keep in touch, but their gratitude discomfited him, and then, of course, there was never any time. Mike, a computer whiz, was on the West Coast with his family, and Steven had been there only once in five years, and that was because of a potential investor in southern California. Mike and his wife had three stepping-stone sons—one, two, and four years of age; and Steven had never seen them except for snapshots.

Bobby, who was now Robert to everyone but his brothers, was an attorney with an Atlanta law firm that worked him endlessly. They touched base by telephone occasionally and said they would meet, at least for a drink, but something always interfered, and now Steven realized it had been him that usually canceled. He had given the excuse of time, but it was more than that: A reluctance to stoke the memories, the horror of that day so long ago.

He wondered whether he had been wrong. He felt a terrible void and emptiness he'd never allowed himself to acknowledge before, but now he knew it had been there, lurking deep within, ready to pounce whenever he lowered his guard.

He had to take more time with his brothers, with

people. After the opening. After Cherokee Hills was successfully on its way. A few weeks. A few months.

Damn Gillian Collins for awakening a loneliness he thought he'd isolated. Damn her for those brown eyes that invaded his very private being. For feeling so soft, for making *him* soft.

Gillian leaned back in her swivel chair and mentally prepared herself to hear his voice. She had to call. Today was Friday, and they had to have the ad into the newspapers no later than Wednesday of next week for inclusion in the daily's Sunday section next week for the following week's opening.

Would it be the old ad Leslie had prepared, or the new one she'd suggested?

Gillian had always been very good at reading the minds of clients, but Steven Morrow was a puzzle. She wondered whether she would ever completely understand him.

Her stomach roiled as she thought about his kiss last night, and abrupt departure. Her body still ached from some kind of unmet anticipation. She had waited nearly thirty years to feel this way, and then she had to fall for a stiff-necked businessman who was more stone than human.

She winced at the thought. She was probably the only thirty-year-old virgin left in the world, and it wasn't for lack of trying. On her part and on that of others. As she embraced everything in life, she had also wanted to know the greatest secret of all, but something in her had always drawn back at the last minute. The magic, the want, had never truly been there with the other men she'd dated. And then, she knew, part of it had been her upbringing. Her mother and father had always been in love, were still in love, and Gillian had never been willing to settle for anything less. She kissed and flirted and enjoyed, but she had also been waiting, and she'd almost given up.

Waiting for *him*? God help her!

She slammed her appointment book down on her desk and looked over toward Leslie's desk, wishing she were here, wishing her partner could take back Steven Morrow, wishing she, Gillian, would never see him again.

Liar!

She picked up the telephone.

"Morrow," he said curtly into the phone when his secretary buzzed him that someone was on the line.

"Hi." Gillian's voice was lazily sexy, as it always seemed to be, and Steven felt his insides tighten. He'd been back in his office only a few moments when the call came, but he knew he'd been waiting for it, that it seemed hours instead of minutes. He'd half expected her to call and cancel their contract after his appalling behavior last night.

His voice softened despite his best intentions not to allow it to do that, not to repeat his fumbles. "Hi," he managed.

There was a silence at the other end, at both ends,

and he heard his own sigh. He could see her in his mind's eye, the silky dark hair falling over the side of her face, the earrings dangling, the eyes endlessly deep and full of lights. She was probably tapping a pencil against her desk with that energy, that bubbling zest she had.

"The ad . . . ?" Her voice was subdued a little, and Steven felt regret for it. Gillian Collins should never be subdued, and he certainly didn't want to be the cause of it.

"We'll go with your version," he said. "Can you get me a final proof on Monday?"

Gillian hesitated. The graphic artist would have to work this weekend, but that certainly had happened before. "I think so. What should I tell Sergei?"

"Plan A, B, or C, you mean?"

There was amusement in his voice now, and she felt a ripple of warmth run through her. "Yep."

"B, I think," he said. There was a pause, and then a warning. "Gillian, I don't want it to overpower the rest of the activities."

"I can alert the radio and television stations, then?"

"Yep," he said, and the amusement was even more evident as he used her own irreverent term. "But in moderation, yes?"

There was another pause. "Yours is but to command," she finally said lightly.

Steven found himself chuckling. There was always that underlying challenge whenever he talked to her. No matter how hard he tried to steel himself, her sassy sense of humor always found penetration someplace. "I doubt that," he retorted drolly, all his good intentions shot to hell again. He'd meant to be impersonal, terse. He was good at that. Usually.

"I'll see you Monday, then," he said.

"Steven . . . ?"

Her voice was tentative, and he found himself clutching the phone tightly. He'd wanted to ask her out over the weekend, but caught himself in time, only to have her do it for him.

"A friend, a client of mine, is performing at the Comedy Club tonight. Would you like to go?"

His gut tightened. A comedy club. He'd never been to one, had never wanted to go. And who was the "friend"? Unfamiliar jealousy ripped through him.

The silence lengthened until it was painful. "What time?" he asked finally.

There was something like a sigh on the other end of the line. Regret? "Eight?"

"Would you like to eat first?" Steven found himself saying.

"Don't you have to work?" There was the slightest tease in her voice.

"Yes." *But someone is interfering with it.* Perhaps he could get it out of his system tonight. He was sure he would hate a comedy club.

She laughed, and he thought how pleasant it sounded, how addictive, how contagious. He wanted to smile even now. "Dinner sounds wonderful."

"Six-thirty then," he said. "Perhaps we could tie

up some loose ends on the opening." The last was for his benefit, he knew.

"I thought there must be strings someplace."

"Of course," he admitted.

"You'll like it."

There was a pregnant pause.

"You will," she insisted.

"Six-thirty," he said.

How could you pack so much life into one slender bundle, he wondered as he watched her across the small table at the Comedy Club.

She was beautiful tonight, her eyes bright, her dark hair fairly glowing in the low lights of the club. She was wearing bright red, a blouse and skirt, both decorated with a green and gold Indian design. She looked exotic and lovely, like a butterfly among moths. Lorelei would have looked lifeless next to her.

He wanted to lean over and kiss her, to push back the lock of long hair falling over her forehead. He studied her features as she laughed at the act currently onstage. They were not beautiful, taken separately. Her cheekbones were too high, her nose too straight, her mouth too wide. It was the pure energy and delight in her, he thought, that made her so attractive, so irresistible.

He made his mouth smile when he heard laughter, but he wasn't really interested in the performing stand-up comedian. He was much more interested in the mobility of her features, of the spontaneous laugh and the quick grin. He had never been quite so fascinated with watching a face change before, but then he was fascinated with everything about her.

They had gone to a small French restaurant for dinner, one where he'd entertained clients and investors before. They knew him and took good care of them. When he'd said they had to rush, their orders had appeared quickly.

But he didn't even taste the food. He'd asked about the print ad, about changes in the proposed radio ads. A special flyer about the circus would be inserted into a program to be given out at the opening. He was amazed at her efficiency, even though he knew he shouldn't be. Not now.

No one played with more joy than she and yet, when required, her mind was sharp and precise.

She was playing now, trying to lead him onto the playground, but he no longer felt equipped to participate. Looking at her made him want to, but something inside him hesitated.

"There he is," his companion said with eagerness, and Steven looked up. He hadn't even noticed that the other man had finished. The new performer was young, much younger than his own thirty-eight years, and had a ready smile. Steven felt an unreasonable antagonism.

He sat back, his jaw set, and, despite the giggles and chuckles around him, decided the man was not in the least bit funny. And then the comedian started a monologue on bankers, and his attempt to get a loan, and suddenly Steven's lips were twitching and he heard his own chuckle. Gillian beamed at him, and he felt strangely like he'd been given a gift of great value.

"Good, isn't he?" Gillian said as the man left the stage. "This was his first appearance in a club, and he really needed some moral support. I hope you didn't mind coming."

"He's . . . has he been a client long?" The fruit of jealousy continued to eat at him.

"He's the son of the artist doing your ad," she said with a gleeful look. "Sort of like a little brother. He works days as a banker."

"I take it his fellow bankers haven't heard him," Steven said dryly, and she laughed.

"He swears he's going to quit soon, and try a cross-country tour of comedy clubs. He's been saving like crazy, because they don't pay anything, most of them anyway."

Steven had a sudden flash of insight. "Another freebie?"

Gillian flushed.

He arched an eyebrow. "Am I the only paying client?"

She grinned. "Not exactly. This club is one too."

"And how did you get your friend a spot?"

"That's what I do," she said loftily. "Put people together. Good matches, like you and the circus. The manager here loved him when he auditioned. Otherwise . . ." She shrugged.

"Otherwise you would have found another way," he suggested with a smile pulling at the side of his lips.

"You are a suspicious man, Mr. Morrow."

He sat back and regarded her solemnly. "So far you've already admitted to blackmail, and I suspect you're not above a little bribery," he observed.

"Bribery?"

"Dinner last night?" Despite a light tone, there was the slightest question in his eyes.

Gillian met his gaze levelly. "You don't give me much credit, Mr. Morrow. If I was going to bribe someone, I think I would use something better than macaroni."

Her smile was gone, and the mood between them had suddenly become strained, combative. Steven knew he was responsible, knew that some devil inside was urging him on. But he also knew he was beginning to care too much about Gillian Collins, and he couldn't dismiss that jealousy he'd felt at seeing her enthusiasm when her friend was performing. Christ, he'd been used once by a woman, and he'd sworn never to let another get close to him again, to have that kind of power. And Gillian Collins was coming close to having that. Witness him coming here tonight.

"Let's go," he said abruptly.

Gillian nodded, and the room seemed to chill. The lights in her eyes had dimmed, and the slightest frown pulled at her mouth. It looked totally out of place.

"The bill?"

"On the house," she said. "Consider it another bribe." This time she didn't hide her anger.

"Gillian . . ."

But she was no longer sitting, and he had to hurry to catch her as she disappeared out the door.

Gillian fumed. She'd known from the moment she'd invited him to the club it was a mistake. But the words had just tumbled out over the phone, the result of wanting to see him and the need to watch him smile.

Billy Champion, the owner of the club, was her best client, just as Steven Morrow had been Leslie's. He was fun to work with because he knew talent and was open to new ideas. His acts were always among the best in Atlanta, and she had been delighted when he liked Cal Caesar, who was a naturally funny person. Gillian had known Cal as long as she'd known his mother, Lucy, who had worked with them as a graphic artist five years. She'd heard Cal's routine about bankers several times, and she'd been the one to urge him to develop it and audition.

Stupidly, she'd thought Steven Morrow might appreciate Cal's wry sense of humor and the way he so accurately pricked the establishment to which he belonged. Maybe she hoped it would be contagious. Idiot, she categorized herself. *He* was impossible. Suspicious. Guarded. There was a dark side to him that she just couldn't penetrate.

And then she thought of his smile during Cal's performance. Such a fleeting smile that understood and appreciated, until that damn guard took over again.

Well, he could hide behind it all he wanted. She knew better than to batter her head against a stone wall.

"Gillian." He had caught up with her and grabbed her arm. She hated the way it made her skin tingle. The pull on her arm forced her to stop and turn around. In the flashing lights of the club's marquee, she saw his face, the handsome face now filled with some emotion she couldn't quite identify. "I'm sorry," he said, his hand dropping from her arm. His voice was so strained, she wondered if he'd ever said the words before. She doubted it. She felt an unwanted tenderness seep through her. He had a dark side, but there was light too . . . when he allowed it.

"You can be an ass," she said suddenly.

"So I've heard," he said, "but never quite so directly." His lips twitched in that intriguing way that always touched her in some odd, private place.

"Too bad," she retorted.

"You're making up for it." He smiled slightly, but it was a searching, vulnerable type of expression.

"You're suspicious, bad tempered, and . . ." She hesitated, trying to think of the best word.

"Pompous?"

She tipped her head slightly. "No . . . not pompous." He could never be that, not with his often quick wit, occasional self-mockery and that . . . rare gentleness at times.

"Insufferable?"

"That qualifies."

"I don't think I dare go on."

"Oh, I think you should. A little self-examination is good for the soul."

"But not the ego."

"Oh, I think your ego can withstand it."

"I think that's another admonition. Am I really that bad?"

"I don't think you want an answer to that, Mr. Morrow."

His eyes flashed with silver, and Gillian realized that the bite had gone out of the exchange, and they had fallen back to the teasing challenge which had been so uniquely theirs from the beginning, since they first had dinner at the Italian restaurant. The anger had dissolved in the apology, and the air between them was charged again, full of energy and intensity and power. Gillian's legs trembled at the strength of it, at the way he'd completely diffused her anger and filled her again with anticipation and excitement.

"I *am* sorry," he said. "I seem to do and say everything wrong when I'm with you. You unsettle me in ways I don't really understand."

Coming from Steven Morrow, the admission was astounding. It would be from any man, but particularly this one who kept so much of himself hidden. But instead of showing weakness, it reflected a strength that rocked her. It was pure, open honesty. A very painful honesty. She saw that in his face, in the hard, scarred granite face that she wanted so badly to touch.

And with the same honesty he'd given her, she did. Her hand went up and touched the edge of his mouth and hesitated there. "You keep surprising me, Mr. Morrow."

"You?" he asked wryly. His lips caught her finger and nibbled on it. They were both mindless of people going in and out of the club. He raised his eyebrow in that way that could be termed, at different times, either supercilious or adorable. Now, Gillian thought, it was adorable.

"Would you like to go back in and say hello to your clients?"

It was yet another apology, and she thought no one did it quite as gracefully as he had, even if he didn't have much practice.

"Cal, perhaps," she said, knowing how anxious the young banker would be despite the obvious crowd approval following his performance.

"He *was* good," Steven said with a roguish expression that was mind-drugging. It wasn't even grudgingly said, Gillian noted with interest.

Steven had been incredibly charming after they'd reentered the Comedy Club, more than she'd ever seen him. It was yet another side of him, and she wondered how deep that particular trait ran. Charm was obviously something he could turn off and on like an electric light. It could be just as bright too.

He had congratulated and complimented Cal, who had been looking for them inside after taking off his makeup, and invited him to join them for a drink. With no trace of his earlier irritation or impatience, he was gracious and interested and soon had Cal discussing his dreams for a future in comedy. He drew him out, like a pump, and Gillian sat there amazed. In a few moments he'd found out more about Cal than she had in months, and she was pretty darn good at doing that.

When they were leaving, Steven turned to Cal and held out his hand. "Go for it," he said with an intensity that surprised Gillian. "Go for the dream, or you'll live with regret all your life."

They were silent most of the way home. Perhaps, Gillian thought, because they were both wondering what came next, perhaps because of the sizzling emotions that made the air explosive, as if a word would detonate it.

He took her hand as they left the car, and when they reached the door, he pulled her to him. "I'll go if you want me to." It was a question, and Gillian merely shook her head. The last thing she wanted now was for him to leave.

Once inside, he leaned down and greeted Spenser and waited as Gillian let the dog outside.

"Drink?"

He shook his head. He never had more than two drinks when he was driving, and he'd consumed those at the Comedy Club. In record speed.

"Coffee then?"

"Sounds good." He needed something in his hands, something to divert his mind.

Gillian disappeared into the kitchen, and he went to the door and looked out. The sky was very clear, the fall air fresh and crisp. Spenser was wandering about, his nose close to the ground as he searched out his particular latrine. Steven had to smile at the concentration. If only human life was so simple.

He waited until Spenser finished and held the door open for him as the dachshund waddled inside, climbed in the beanbag chair and made himself happily at home. The picture of total contentment! He felt envy. This place was a home, not because of its size or address, but because of the woman who lived and loved here.

"He's shamelessly spoiled," Gillian said, and he turned and watched her come into the room, her hands holding two large coffee cups.

He looked at the coffee. "Do you shamelessly spoil everyone?"

"I try."

He believed it. He took a cup and walked over to the sound system and looked over the collection of music.

She followed him. "What's your pleasure?"

"You *do* spoil everyone. You pick."

"I warn you. I'm also a shameless romantic."

"You?" he scoffed with a mock disbelieving look.

"As far as music goes," she amended, although she was afraid her eyes were saying something else.

"Now I would have taken you for a rock addict."

"Good rock," Gillian said, "but now I'm in the mood for soft and comforting."

"Comforting?"

"It's been a . . ."

". . . hell of a night," he completed.

Her eyes had moved from the sound system to him, and their eyes locked on each other. Why did he always do this to her? Make her forget everything in the world other than his presence? Other than the rapid beating of her heart, and the blood pulsing in all the places it shouldn't?

And then he took her coffee cup and placed both of them on a table. Music forgotten, she walked into his arms as though it was the most natural thing in the world.

She felt his lips against her cheek, brushing kisses along her skin, and she knew that innate gentleness that he usually hid so well. Every touch, every kiss was a caress, sweet and fine and intoxicating.

His lips reached her ear and nibbled, his tongue playing along the lobe, inciting a riot of sensations inside her. "Gillian," he whispered, and his breath sent new waves of pleasure roaring through her.

Gillian's arms went up around him, and she turned her head to meet his lips. It was suddenly as if the world caught fire and she'd been swept into its center. The gentleness was gone, and hunger was there: Raw, primitive hunger. His lips pressed down on hers, and she answered with the same naked need.

She heard him groan, and she didn't know whether it was one of denial or simply the physical agony of their bodies stretching and bending toward each other, seeking. She looked up, and his eyes glittered with a brightness she had never seen there before.

Gillian clung to him as his mouth ground into hers, his lips asking hers to open, and they did. She felt his tongue enter her mouth, deliciously voracious as it tantalized, awakening every erotic nerve in her. Her whole body was singing a new mesmerizing song, and she was swaying to its magic.

And what magic it was! Now she knew what she had been waiting for. Why she had been waiting. She had known instinctively it should be something wonderful, something like this. And she wasn't going to let it go.

His lips moved from her lips to her neck, nuzzling, murmuring her name. It sounded so lyrical the way he said it, the way he drew it out as if reluctant to give it up.

There was a growing ache in her stomach, in the core of her, a craving, a longing she knew only he could relieve. "Steven . . . Steve . . ."

His groan came louder. "For Christ's sake, Gillian, I . . ."

"You talk too much," she said, realizing that her voice was husky.

She heard a sudden muffled laughter from inside his chest. And then his mouth was back on hers, and he wasn't talking at all, and neither was she.

EIGHT

Gillian was vaguely aware of leading Steven to the bedroom. Leading. Accompanying. Following. She didn't know. She didn't care.

She was in a trance of feelings. Overwhelming feelings composed of equal parts of exquisite need and emotional expectation, of sensations so strong that nothing existed for her but Steven Morrow, and the feel and scent and aura of him.

Her world had always been full of color, but never before had she experienced this kind of physical intensity, when even a touch made her ache, and a breath against her skin made her shiver with pleasure.

Was this love?

It had to be, because she'd never known anything like it, could not even have imagined anything like it.

They reached the bed, and she felt his hands start to unbutton her blouse, and then stop. "Are you sure?"

"Yes," she said softly and emphasized her answer

by standing up on tiptoe and kissing him, her tongue entwining with his. His mouth clasped hers tightly, his arms squeezing her so tightly to him that she felt they were already one. Her body was consumed with need of him, of heat and sensations and hunger. "Yes," she whispered again, as his lips went down to her neck. "Oh yes."

His hands released her and fumbled with the rest of the buttons to her blouse and then her bra, and she felt his lips on her breast, felt the incredible sensation as the nipple hardened and ached with his touch. She shivered as his mouth played with it, his tongue teasing and drawing circles until she thought she could no longer stand the sweet pain of it, the hunger it spurred.

She found her own hands pulling at his tie and then unbuttoning his shirt, her fingers touching the gold wiry hair that sprung from his chest, that hard muscular chest that now was both warm and moist. She moved her head so it rested on his heart, and she could hear its beat, steady and strong.

Gillian wasn't exactly sure how they wrested the remainder of their clothes from each other, but then they were on the bed, and he was kissing her, his mouth moving down her body, making her glow and murmur little sighs of pleasure. Her body sizzled with every touch, aching for more, yet still savoring every second of what was happening.

He turned away for a moment and fumbled in his pants' pocket, and then after a brief pause turned back to her. His hand moved down to the triangle at her legs and touched and caressed, and when her sigh turned to a groan he lifted himself above her and teased her with his arousal, moving seductively around the entrance to her womanhood until, in agony, she reached around him and pulled him down to her.

He entered with a deep thrust, and she couldn't help but cry out at the sudden pain. He stopped, and she felt his whole body stiffened. "God," she heard him say.

The pain was eclipsed now by her need for him, and her hands pulled him down again as her body arched up, seeking to bring him back to her, to reestablish that communion they'd had. "It's all right," she said softly. "Don't go."

He began to move again, this time slowly, tenderly until their hunger matched again, and she caught his rhythm and responded with movements of her own. Gillian throbbed with delicious feelings, with the instinctive responses that she knew brought him deeper and deeper into the core of her until she thought she would go mad with desire and passion and raw, naked greed for fulfillment. His movements became stronger, more frantic, and her own met his until they were both racing, racing toward something Gillian knew had always been there, waiting for her. And then passion exploded deep inside her, sending torrents of pleasure ripping through her, flooding her body and mind and soul.

He lay there quietly for several moments. They

both did, letting the aftermath of passion ripple through them, and then very slowly he moved, and lay next to her.

"You were a virgin," he accused.

Gillian surmised quickly it was not a state that particularly pleased him. She lay her head on his chest, again feeling the heartbeat, and his arms went around her, almost reluctantly.

"You don't like virgins?"

His arms tensed. "I avoid them like the plague."

"Now you don't have to avoid me." She tried to make her voice light, but something heavy weighed on her heart.

"Ah, Gillian." He sighed, his hands running up and down her body, bringing it back to stinging anticipation.

"I'm sorry," she said.

"No, you're not," he argued, quite correctly as a matter of fact. "But why . . . ?"

"Why now? Why you?"

"Yeah."

"Would you believe that I decided when I was ten years old that on October twenty first, in this year, I would become . . ." Gillian hunted for exactly the right word. "Deflowered?" She knew he wouldn't accept the real reason, that, God help her, she had fallen in love with him.

She felt that rumbling inside him, that beginning of a chuckle, and she wondered if he was going to let it come all the way out. He did.

She turned her face up and kissed him, feeling his lips twitch.

When she was quite through, he mumbled, "You're a witch."

"Good witch or bad witch?"

"I haven't decided. Do you ever take anything seriously?"

"Oh I take this very seriously. Nothing ever so grand has happened before. Was it grand for you, too, even though . . . ?" She stopped, unable to bear the thought it wasn't good for him too.

"You're a witch?" He finished the sentence.

"No, a virgin."

"Past tense, Miss Collins. You *were* a virgin."

"I know. Isn't it wonderful?"

"No." His voice was stern, as it had been when they'd first met.

"Well, I think so, Mr. Morrow. I like it, I liked it very much." She started nibbling on some of his chest hair, and she felt his arousal again. She still felt full, full of him, yet empty too. Like she wanted him back, wanted to explore all those sensations again.

"Gillian!"

"Steven!" she replied in a tone mockingly familiar to his. Her mouth reached up to stop any protest he might have. And she did. His mouth was suddenly hungry on hers, and his body was wrapping itself around hers. She knew what to do now; she knew exactly what to do.

❧——————❧

Steven lay there, Gillian asleep in his arms. His mind was in turmoil. He'd never experienced anything like the past few hours.

His body was sated, but just thinking about Gillian made it ache again. He wondered whether that particular pain would ever go away.

She was so spontaneous, so incredibly free in her passion, in wanting to experience everything, in every way. She gave totally, hiding nothing, holding back nothing. She filled him with a kind of joy he'd never known before.

And she scared the hell out of him.

A virgin. The last thing he'd expected. Perhaps because of her headlong rush into things, the way she embraced life, and even dared it to disagree with her.

A virgin. The implications were astounding. He wasn't sure how old she was, but he did have her résumé tucked in his file, a part of the proposal presented by Leslie. She had to be nearly thirty. And God knew she had to have any number of chances and offers.

That she had chosen him was both humbling and frightening. He wasn't good with relationships. He never had been. He'd always been too busy surviving, helping his family survive. Even then it had been his sense of responsibility rather than real connection to individuals. He'd never really been able to depend on anyone, trust anyone, particularly after Lorelei, the one time he had experimented with that particular vulnerability.

He had vowed to himself he wouldn't make that

mistake again. And now he didn't even know whether he could. He'd always been afraid that the taint of violence that had always run in his family might someday surface in him. And now he'd been alone too long to know how to share even the smallest piece of himself.

Yet perhaps he had done that tonight. He had never quite made love like this before. With a kind of aching tenderness that reached beyond physical pleasure.

He had given pleasure before. He knew how to make love. He just didn't know how to give it.

Damn her.

But she felt so good in his arms. He looked down at the untroubled face, at the long eyelashes shielding those incredible eyes of hers, and the soft skin of her cheeks against the dark silkiness of her hair. His heart speeded, and he felt something catch in his throat as he watched her breathe, a smile of contentment on those lovely lips. He closed his eyes, feeling himself wrapped in pain. This would never work. They were too different. She gave everything, and he didn't know how to give anything. He would eventually crush her, and her spirit, and himself in the process.

This could never happen again. Never.

He closed his eyes, willing himself to sleep, but another part of him objected, wanting instead to hold her, and watch her. And so he did.

Gillian woke slowly, sensuously. She stretched like a cat and wanted to purr as she felt Steven next to her, savored the now familiar sensation of skin against skin. She opened her eyes and saw his, grave and serious, fixed on her.

"Good morning, Steven. It's a glorious day, isn't it?" Her voice fondled his name, and a kind of painful pleasure ripped through him.

His arms went around her, and she cuddled up in them, relishing the warmth and strength of his body, the protectiveness of his hold.

"You haven't even seen it yet," he observed practically.

"I don't have to. Even if it were pouring down rain, it would be lovely, every drop a crystal just for us."

She moved her head, so her lips could reach his, and she kissed him, tenderly at first and then with growing fervor, or perhaps desperation as she saw the set of his jaw.

"Steven?"

There was so much uncertainty in her voice that guilt nearly consumed him, and his arms tightened around her. "You're beautiful, Gillian Collins."

"So are you."

"Broken nose and all?" His tone was rueful.

"Gives you character."

"Then I have lots of that."

"Tell me about football."

There was a silence, then a sigh. "What do you want to know?"

Gillian knew she was treading on sensitive ground, but he'd said so little about himself and his past. "Why? Why did you play? You don't seem to talk about it much."

His voice was full of resignation as he answered. "It seemed the fastest, easiest route to success." He hesitated, then added wryly, "I thought."

"You didn't enjoy it?"

He thought for a moment. For some reason, he hadn't really analyzed the way he felt about those years. The aftermath of his ill-fated career had smothered the good times. "I suppose I did," he said finally. "I'm competitive. I've always been competitive, and there's nothing sweeter than winning."

"And nothing more bitter than losing?"

Her comment startled him. For some reason he hadn't expected it. "It's not whether you win or lose, it's the way you play the game," he said in a singsong voice full of mockery. "That's usually said by winners."

Cynicism weighed down his words, and Gillian felt herself shiver. "And there's no joy at all in the playing?"

"I suppose it depends on the stakes, Miss Collins," he said. "The stakes in my case was a pro career. I had to be better than anyone else, even if I wasn't that good an athlete. I had to work harder."

"And you still do," she said. "Work harder than anyone. Why? To prove a point?"

She was crawling inside his head, and he wasn't

sure he liked it. He had never talked to anyone like this before.

"Enough about me," he said. "I want to know more about Gillian Collins."

"But you're much more interesting."

"Ah, but you've implied I'm a workaholic. There's nothing interesting about workaholics."

"You're much more than that. When you allow yourself."

But any sting in her words was negated by the way her body snuggled comfortably into his.

"Mmmmmm, you think so?"

"Oh yes," she sighed happily, her meaning only too clear, but he wasn't going to let it happen again. Not now.

Or was he?

Steven had never been so undisciplined in his life, had never given in to weakness, but he was no stronger now than a leaf in the wind. She had merely to touch him, to look as if he were something so very special, and he was putty in her hands.

Well, perhaps not putty, he thought as he felt himself growing hard again.

Was he winning now? Or losing?

For the first time in his life, he didn't care as once more his body became part of hers.

Gillian pulled a T-shirt over her head and left the bed to make some coffee. It was all he wanted, he said, when she'd offered to make breakfast.

He stretched and got up after her, slipping on his shorts and slacks, and then his somewhat wrinkled shirt which had been lying where they'd so frantically discarded it. He needed as many clothes between them as possible.

Dismayed, he looked at the time on her clock. It was nine o'clock, well into his usual workday. It was Saturday. But he didn't take Saturdays off, or treat them any differently than any other workday. And he had a great deal to do, particularly badger the builders and contractors into finishing their jobs in time for the opening. Instead, he'd been lolling around in bed with . . . a virgin. Ex-virgin. He winced at the thought.

He wandered into the kitchen and leaned against the doorjamb. He liked watching her. She was taking cups down from the overhead cabinets, reaching up as she did, and the T-shirt outlined the slim, energetic body.

As she twisted around and saw him, her hands remained in midair, and then she smiled slowly, and shook her head in a deliberate motion as if chastising him.

"You were supposed to wait there."

"I've work to do."

"I was afraid of that," she said. "But at least stay for coffee."

She had run a comb through her hair, but that was all, yet she seemed to glow in the sun that flooded the room. Her coloring, even without makeup, was vivid, her cheeks tinged with a healthy blush and her eyes bright with life. He looked around a kitchen he'd barely noticed the night before. Like her, it was bright and lively. A stained glass mobile hung in the window, bright yellow curtains were pushed back to allow the sun entrance. They matched the seat cushions and an arrangement of dried flowers that sat on a table. The cat was contentedly eating a bowl of food as Spenser eyed him enviously.

Steven thought of his own condominium. The best that could be said about it and the furniture was cold utilitarian.

Here, a kind of warmth rushed through him, a sense of belonging he'd never felt anyplace before. He wondered what it would be like to wake up every day to this kind of . . . environment. Would he ever get to work?

Obviously not, if this morning was any indication. He berated himself for his total lack of discipline, of resolve. But he felt so good inside, so warm and . . . happy. God help him.

"Milk or sugar?"

"Huh?" The question jerked him back to reality, but still he had to think a moment for it to penetrate. He shook his head. "Just black."

"I should have known that."

"Why?"

She crooked her head to one side. "You just seem like a black coffee type of person."

He stepped away from the wall and took the cup. "I don't think I know how to take that."

She grinned. "No frills, no nonsense."

"And you, Miss Collins. How do you take your coffee?"

"Black," she admitted.

"I never would have taken you for a black coffee type of person," he said with a smug expression.

"Oh I have my plain, no-nonsense moments."

He raised an eyebrow.

"I do," she insisted.

The eyebrow went up even higher in challenge.

"I'm very practical about some things. Particularly my business."

"When it doesn't interfere with Russian circuses?" Steven heard the words, and knew instantly from the way her eyes clouded that they hadn't come out right. He had meant it teasingly, but they sounded condescending instead, even critical. Damn, he didn't have much experience with teasing, with light patter. He didn't know how. Some of the warmth he'd felt drained away.

"I'd better go," he said abruptly.

She didn't say anthing, merely looked at him with those eyes he could drown in. He found himself lifting his empty hand to touch a silky strand of hair and then move to her cheek where it hovered a fraction of a second.

It was an apology of sorts. "You are a bewitching young woman, Gillian Collins."

"Can I bewitch you to stay a few minutes longer?" She said the words lightly, but her eyes said something else, pleaded with him.

He shook his head. "I must go." At the disappointment in her face, he hesitated. "Would you like to have dinner tonight?"

Gillian tipped her head and looked directly up at him. "You don't owe me anything."

He shook his head in disagreement. "I do, but that's not why I asked you."

"Then why?"

She was trying to make him say something he didn't want to say, something like "I want to be with you." He did, dear God, how he wanted that. But for some reason he couldn't say the words. He couldn't put that dangerous fact into words.

"Would you?" he said instead, ignoring the question.

Gillian nodded, a thoughtful look on her face. "What time?"

"Seven?"

"I'll be ready."

He hesitated just a fraction of a second longer, wanting to lean down and kiss her but afraid if he did it would deepen into something else, and he would never leave.

"Good-bye," he said stiffly and turned, walking swiftly to the front door. How he hated to leave this place and all its warmth, but then he resolutely opened the door and strode to his pickup. He didn't like the feeling of emptiness he had as he started the ignition and pulled out of the driveway.

NINE

Steven couldn't work.

He'd never had that problem before, and now he sat at his desk, twiddling a pencil like an errant school-boy, and pondered the puzzle.

He didn't particularly like the answer forming in his mind. He didn't like being afraid of something that felt so right.

One of his brothers had defeated the odds that haunted all the four brothers, the fear that a strain of violence tainted the family. Mike had a great family, but Robert had, in one drunken moment, expressed the fears Steven had never been able to put into words. It had been mentioned once, and never a second time.

But now they became real again. And Steven knew why he worked so damned hard. There was nothing else in his life, nothing to hurry home to, but empti-ness. And he was too damned scared of himself to change it.

He had accomplished a little this morning. He had

driven out to Cherokee Hills and put the fear of God into a few contractors, promising that they would never work for him, or anyone he knew, if they didn't meet the contract. He realized he was taking out personal frustration on them, and he didn't like himself for doing it, and, again, it rang the warning bells inside his head.

So he'd returned to the office, thinking to complete some paperwork. But he couldn't concentrate. His mind's eye kept wandering back to Gillian and the happy, sleepy, sexy way she'd looked this morning. And the way he'd felt.

He cursed, jerked back the chair and stood up. A drive. A drive would remove all those cobwebs in his brain. He locked the office and strode out to his pickup, trying to decide where to go.

And he found himself driving toward the motel where the circus was staying. Turn around, part of him said. But he couldn't. Something deep inside was guiding him, and it wouldn't be denied.

Gillian spent a lazy morning. She'd taken her coffee and the newspaper that had been delivered that morning, and crawled back into the bed that still whispered softly of Steven's musky scent.

She tried to read, but the words all blurred. She could only think of the way her body had felt last night and this morning, and the way it still felt. She could only see the way he looked as he made love, the cool gray eyes smoky with passion and emotion. He was like a very deep pool of water, with magnificent underwater caves just waiting for discovery and exploration.

She wriggled, feeling all the new sensuality of her body as it reacted even to the thought of him. The cool sheets felt extraordinarily good against her body, and her hand rested where Steven had been only hours ago. Just a few hours, and she would see him again.

Gillian knew she should get up. Her efficiency this week had reached ground zero. She needed to put together updated news releases on the opening, which meant a visit to the circus to finalize exactly which acts would appear.

She sighed contentedly, thinking of those wonderful gray eyes, that grave expression that rarely gave way to a smile, but when it did, wow, batten down the hatches. She wanted to make him smile. She wanted to make him laugh. She wanted to make him happy.

In fact, Gillian knew suddenly, inexplicably but quite absolutely, that she had never wanted anything so badly in her life.

The first thing Gillian saw as she drove up to the motel was the blue pickup truck, and Steven Morrow leaning against it as he watched a group of acrobats practice.

She was sure no one else had seen him, for if they had, Sergei would have besieged him. Steven was slightly hidden by the truck, his stance relaxed. She

could only see his profile, and she could tell nothing
from his expression. But then she rarely could. Until
last night when he'd made love to her.

This morning, however, he was his usual inscruta-
ble self. But he was obviously very absorbed in what he
was watching, for he had not noticed her, and he usually noticed everything.

She parked her car, and walked over to the pickup,
moving almost silently to stand beside him. "Hi," she
said softly.

He whirled around, surprise obvious in his expression, and something else, too, but Gillian couldn't
quite decipher it.

"Gillian!"

"I'm afraid so," she said with no trace of regret in
her cheerful voice. "I didn't expect you, either."

There was a question in the comment, and
Steven's expression was a little like a boy caught filch-
ing a lollipop.

He shrugged off the implied question. "I was out
this way," he said. "And you?"

"Working for my slave-driving client." She
grinned.

He arched that eyebrow of his, the one that sent
her heart spinning out of control. Her mind too. Un-
fortunately. And now, by golly, her body. It was already trembling.

"That bad?"

"Nope. In some ways, he can be quite . . . nice."

"Nice?" Mock outrage tinged his reply as the
barest twinkle glimmered in his eyes.

Gillian was entranced, as she always was when that humor darted out so unexpectedly at times. "Well, a few other things too," she admitted. "I didn't want to get out of bed this morning, and leave where you'd been." It was a totally shameless thing to say, but Gillian had always done that: Her mouth just popped open and expressed her feeling, no matter how unwise it might be.

His expression softened, and she thought how handsome he was when he didn't try so hard to be stern. "Do you always say exactly what you think?"

"Yes," she said. "Do you *ever*?"

"Hardly ever," he said with a twitch of his lips.

"Are you good at lessons?"

"Dismal."

"Then I have my work cut out for me."

"It depends on your goal."

"Do you always think in terms of goals?"

"Don't you?"

Gillian shook her head. How could she explain that she didn't believe in setting goals. She simply believed in living each day for its own sake, doing the best she could. Goals locked you in. Or, to use a cliché, kept you from seeing the forest for the trees. At least that was her philosophy, such as it was. She'd come to the conclusion that she might be the only one in the world that felt that way. Her partner, Leslie, had been a goal setter too. Gillian had just ignored them, and went her own way. Sometimes, she wondered if she were the odd one, but then dismissed the idea since she had no intention of changing anyway.

"Goals are restrictive," she said finally with a defiant lift to her chin.

"They're productive," he corrected.

"Not for some of us."

"Because you haven't tried."

"Just like you don't try expressing what you think."

"Touché, Miss Collins."

Gillian grinned. "Let's start lesson one."

"If I cooperate, then you have to try goal setting."

"Okay. I have a goal," Gillian said with a wickedly sensuous smile that made him know exactly what that goal was.

"That wasn't what I had in mind," he said, then grinned himself. "Not precisely," he amended. "Except maybe. A little. A lot. God, I'm babbling." A perplexed, disbelieving expression passed over his face.

"Good lesson one," Gillian said. "Now for two." She took his hand. "I want you to meet someone."

Still dazed at his own confusion, Steven allowed himself to be led into the motel office.

They went to a house phone, and he stood back as Gillian spoke into it. He couldn't hear what she was saying, but he enjoyed watching her. He always enjoyed watching her. Her whole body spoke. She was never still, and energy always radiated from her, energy and that endearing honesty that was so uniquely hers.

When she put the receiver down, there was triumph on her face. "Let's go out to the pool," she said.

At the moment, he would probably have followed her to hell. She had such a mischievous, purposeful look on her face that more than his lips twitched. His heart did too.

The pool was full of Russians. Steven had never seen so many fit bodies, and he watched as they churned through the water with purpose. He felt something of Gillian's empathy for them, stranded in a foreign country and living on charity when they were so obviously skilled and among the best in the world at what they did.

There had to be a kind of hopelessness in their situation, and he knew about hopelessness.

"Steven."

He took his eyes from the pool and turned them back to Gillian. Two other people had joined them, Sergei and someone Steven didn't recognize. But the stranger would have been hard to identify in any event because his face was painted with black and white.

"This is Konstantin . . . a mime."

Konstantin made a series of facial and hand movements indicating his pleasure at meeting Steven, and then went into another series which translated easily into gratitude and appreciation for his help.

Steven recalled Gillian's own hand movements, and how much they, and her own face, always showed, along with her words. She would make a great mime, too, but he wouldn't like for her to lose her speech, that spontaneous honesty that was so totally engaging. Still, it was amazing how much he comprehended of what was being said to him now by the mime.

She was gesturing herself now, communicating silently to the mime, and Konstantin was grinning at her, and then him.

"He would like to teach you," she said, "in appreciation for your help, but I told him you were too much of a stone face."

Another challenge, by God, and he was tempted as he looked into her laughing face, but even as the aberrant thought crossed his mind, he dismissed it, although a little reluctantly. There was no time for such nonsense.

Still, a part of him said, it might be . . . interesting. Even fun.

Later.

Which is what he said. "Perhaps later," he replied, "after the grand opening. But thank him."

"You do it," she said.

He felt chased by a tiger who wouldn't let go until he complied. But how? How could he say thank you when he did not speak Russian and everyone was obviously waiting for a gesture? Gillian's eyes were bright, waiting on him, and he suddenly didn't want to disappoint her.

He finally smiled, clasped his hands together in front of his chest and gave a little bow. It was the best he could manage, and he was inordinately pleased when Konstantin beamed in approval, as did Gillian.

Sergei also smiled. "You would make good pupil."

Steven looked at him with skepticism, and then glanced down at his watch. He'd wasted the whole afternoon. For the second time today, he felt as if he were nothing but a hollowed-out log being swept down a raging river. Powerless to stop. He resented the feeling. Yet . . . he really didn't want to leave the enchantment of the circus, of its ageless fantasy, nor Gillian. Especially Gillian.

But it was as if she read his mind this time, for she made apologies to Sergei and Konstantin. "I think we both have to go," she said diplomatically. "I'll be back Monday."

Konstantin looked desolate, an expression magnified by the painted face, and in his own way said farewell and gracefully slid away, Sergei behind him.

Steven turned to Gillian. "I'm not going to push my luck," she said with that gamin smile that always made his heart do flip-flops. "And I really do have some work of my own to do. I'll see you tonight."

And then she, too, was gone, and he stood there for a moment, wondering exactly what had just happened.

As Steven shaved that evening, he wondered where to take Gillian that night. He had never given much thought to a date before, not since college, in any event. He had squired women, of course, many of them, and had taken some to bed.

As a rule, most of his dates had been sleek, model-beautiful women whose appearance had been useful to entertaining and to his business. But none of them had meant anything to him. He had given physical pleasure and received it, no strings attached.

He had usually taken them to very expensive, equally sleek restaurants, often as part of a business evening. But Gillian was different.

He smiled as he considered just how different Gillian was from any woman he'd ever met. As much as he'd been loath to admit it, she did something special for all his internal parts. His heart lifted at her smile, his body tingled at her closeness, his whole being came alive in her presence. Nothing like that had ever happened before. Nor had anything like last night happened before.

He had been told he was a good lover. He knew technically he was; he knew that from responses. But he had never really given before, never held back as he had last night to give her as much pleasure as he could, never kissed or touched with gentleness that only she seemed to find in him. It had felt good, so very good.

Good enough that it had shielded the past.

He shook off the brief cloud, wondering again where to take her. He suspected she wouldn't particularly like the very formal places he frequented for business, and he didn't want to take her to the Italian restaurant. Steven wanted to please her in some special way, even though he realized that Gillian would probably enjoy anything. That was part of her magic, the way she found something wonderful in everything. Even him.

Almost automatically, he reached for one of his suits, noting for the first time that they all looked alike, all gray, and his ties similar. Had he really been in such a rut?

And then he looked around the condominium. One of the women he'd dated had offered to choose his furniture and, busy as he had been, he'd agreed indifferently. It was trendy, chrome and black, and not very comfortable. Sterile. He suddenly wondered if that had been the woman's image of him, or their relationship. He'd stopped dating her before any paintings were added. Thank God.

Steven knotted his tie, suddenly thinking of a small Hungarian restaurant where he'd once met one of his contractors for dinner. He glanced in the mirror and took note of the silly smile on his face. It was disgusting. Still, as he left the apartment, he had the terrible suspicion it was still there.

He was gorgeous. But then, Gillian thought as she opened the door to his knock, he was always gorgeous. How could she have ever thought otherwise. His thick sandy hair, the steady gray eyes, the facial features she once thought austere and stern were all now incredibly appealing.

He had a somewhat perplexed half smile on his face as she tipped up on her toes and kissed him. "I've been wanting to do that all day," she said after she had satisfactorily finished.

"I've been wanting to do something else all day," he retorted.

Gillian knew her expression must resemble that of a cat looking at a giant bowl of cream, because he suddenly grinned, that rare, wonderful smile that jerked her heart inside out. But that was exactly the way she felt, like a lazy sensuous expectant cat. Then she amended that thought. She was definitely not thinking about a bowl of cream.

Spenser had waddled over to him and now barked, demanding acknowledgment at the very least. Steven gave her a rueful look, then bent down, way down, and fondled Spenser's ear, much to the animal's wriggling delight.

"He likes you," Gillian observed happily.

"He'd like a mass murderer if he said a kind word."

"I don't think mass murderers say kind words."

"A smart one would."

"I bow to your knowledge of mass murderers," she said in surrender. More than one person had questioned Spenser's competence as a watchdog.

"Ready to go?"

"I'm not quite sure," Gillian said, hunger battling desire.

"We can always eat Spenser." Steven regarded the dog with a measuring eye.

"I'm ready," Gillian said quickly, but with a smile.

"I'm sure Spenser's grateful."

"Oh, he knows you didn't really mean it."

He looked at her sternly, as if affronted by her disbelief. But now Gillian recognized the look, the one that disguised an oddly whimsical sense of humor.

She looked up at him. "I like you a lot, Mr. Morrow."

"I should hope so after last night."

"I would like you, anyway."

He thought he should be insulted. *Like*, for Christ's sake. He felt a lump of disappointment, even though he knew it was ridiculous. "Like" was all he wanted from a woman. Just the same. . . .

"As you 'like' Spenser?" There was a trace of indignation in the question.

"Hmmmm, you're as cuddly as Spenser."

Steven frowned with dismay as he noted Spenser's wide body. "If you're referring to appearances, maybe we shouldn't go out to dinner, after all."

"Not exactly," Gillian said.

"Then I think I'm even more insulted."

Gillian giggled. "Not that, either."

"All right then," he said, slightly mollified. He leaned down, and his lips brushed hers. "We have to hurry. I have reservations."

And he would never be late, Gillian knew. "Dare I ask where?" she said, looking down at her dress. It was an emerald-green blouse and swirling skirt, with a silver belt emphasizing a small waist and a multicolored scarf adding color at her neck. She still wore the large hoop earrings, but tonight they were silver instead of gold. She looked like an exotic gypsy princess with her shining dark hair and glinting dark brown eyes.

"Nope," he said as he eyed her appreciatively.

"Should I trust you?"

"Nope," he said again.

She stopped their progress to the door with her hand. She looked up at him. "I do, you know," she said quietly, and Steven felt as if someone had pounded him with a sledgehammer. The impact of that simple statement was so incredibly powerful, so terrifying in its implications.

"You shouldn't," he warned her, and the amusement in his voice was gone.

She shook her head in denial of his words, then still holding his hand started forward again. "We have to hurry. You have reservations," she said with a grin, gently mocking his own admonition.

He could do nothing other than follow.

The restaurant, located along a thoroughfare in a northern Atlanta suburb, was everything he remembered even if it did take them forty-five minutes to get there. It had once been a pancake house but some creative soul had transformed it into a dark, intimate little restaurant with high wood booths which gave the impression of privacy. Candles and fresh flowers decorated each table, and violin music played softly through an excellent sound system.

Steven had found the restaurant in the yellow pages and called for reservations just prior to leaving his apartment, which apparently had been wise. A small lounge was packed with waiting would-be patrons.

He was grateful that he'd thought of the restaurant when he saw the delight on her face. "I'd heard of this place," she said, "but I've never been here. It's wonderful."

"Wait until you taste the food," he said. But warmth spread through him at her pleasure.

She shrugged happily. The fact that he had even thought of this place filled her with a bubbling happiness. It had taken an effort to please her. She had been terribly afraid they would go to a country club or some equally formal place. Then she had a terrible thought. "You've been here before?"

"Once . . . with one of my contractors," he said. "His office is around the corner."

Business again. She ought to have known. But it was better than if he'd been here with a woman. She'd felt the bitter bite of jealousy for a moment, something she'd never felt before.

After asking her preference, Steven ordered a bottle of wine, which came with homemade hot bread. The music and wine and delicious aromas filled Gillian with a wonderful sense of well-being.

His eyes were no longer coldly gray, but heated as they watched her, heated and hungry and full of emotion. She deeply regretted the table between them, but reached out her hand across it. Steven took her palm, his thumb running over the back of her hand, stroking and caressing as the current of attraction ran through her body. It was running through his, too, she noted, as a muscle twitched in his cheek.

"I want to know everything there is to know about Steven Morrow," she said finally.

The muscle twitched again. "There isn't much."

"Do you have a family?" she said, ignoring the warning signals now emitting from him like signals from a shortwave. Gillian had sensed long ago he didn't like talking about himself, but the wine made her reckless. She had to know. She needed to know.

The thumb stopped stroking her hand, and he used that hand to pick the wine glass back up. "Two brothers now," he said.

"Where are they?"

"One's in California. The other, Bobby, lives here."

Gillian felt momentary surprise. For some reason, she didn't know why, she'd thought . . .

She didn't know what she'd thought, except that he seemed so alone, such a solitary person. She thought of her own sisters, how much she missed them. "Do you see each other much."

Steven shrugged. "Robert's an attorney, trying to make partner. There's never any time."

"And the other brother?"

"Mike? He's a computer genius."

Gillian knew she should stop, but she couldn't, not now that he was answering her questions. "Your mother and father?"

"Dead," he said flatly.

The food came then, and Gillian saw the relief on his face. She'd never met anyone as reluctant to speak about himself as Steve Morrow, and she was usually very adept at drawing people out. Trying to draw *him* out, though, was like beating a stone wall with a fist. The only casualty was herself. Yet she hungered for more knowledge of him.

The food was as wonderful as the atmosphere.

They both had goulash, which was recommended by the waiter, and it was full of herbs that filled the air with unusual but irresistible smells. The candle flickered across his face, across the thin scar, and the gray eyes that now so fascinated her.

They ate in relative silence, only the softly sweet-sad sounds of the violins, and the murmur of voices at other tables, infringing on the intimacy between them. Their eyes caught and held, but Gillian felt the tension between them: Part magnetic physical attraction, part emotional impact, and a sprinkling of wariness from him. When she looked up and deep into his eyes, she saw raw, naked need, despite his obvious attempts to tame it.

"Steven?"

His fork hesitated in the air, as he looked at her.

It took a measure of courage for her to continue. "What do you want?"

"Want?"

"Next year, five years from now?"

His eyes curtained over. "I thought you were the girl that believed only in today."

"You don't have to remember everything I say," she complained.

"Oh, but I do, Miss Collins. Every word."

"*Every* word?"

"Even about my being an ass. I'm trying to compensate."

"You already compensated for that," she said. "And very well, may I add."

"I'm storing brownie points for next time."

Gillian made a face. "There's going to be *another* time?"

"Quite probably," Steven said, his expression saturnine in the candlelight, the gray eyes smoldering with some unknown, indefinable emotion.

"Why?"

"Such a simple question for such a complicated subject," he said. "Do you believe in dark sides of people, Miss Collins?" There was suddenly an intensity about his own question that sent shivers down her back.

"Of course," she said after a moment's thought. "To some people."

"And how do you tell if there is?"

"I don't think *you* have a dark side, if that's what you mean."

His gaze bored into her now, and the shivers grew more pronounced. Something was troubling him, something very strong, and she knew it had something to do with the way he bottled up all his thoughts, all his emotions.

"Now me," she said, trying to break that sudden ominous strain between them. "I have a temper that makes Leslie despair."

"I know," he said wryly as some of the tension seemed to seep from his body. "I saw it last night. But that's not exactly what I meant."

"What did you mean?"

He shrugged suddenly, and he shifted the mask back on. He picked up the bottle. "Some more wine?"

Gillian knew that brief trek into his mind had been abruptly barricaded. "Do you ever let anyone in?"

He didn't ask her to explain. He knew exactly what she was asking. Steven shook his head slowly.

"Why?"

"I don't know how," he said simply, and Gillian thought, in that one minute, that her heart would break for him.

TEN

The interior of the car fairly sizzled with heat and expectation.

Following that one vulnerable glimpse into himself, Steven had kept the conversation light. But there was nothing light about the currents running between them. They were like fused dynamite, just waiting for a match to ignite.

Despite Steven's reticence, Gillian felt closer to him than she had to any man. Perhaps it had been the gentleness with which he'd made love, perhaps those rare glimpses into a very complicated man, one whose rivers ran deeper than even she had imagined.

Perhaps just karma . . . fate . . . destiny, whatever it was called.

Perhaps. Perhaps. Gillian couldn't snuggle up to him as she wanted because of the gear shift, but she did the next best thing: She leaned against the door and watched him, watched the light from the overhead road lamps shadow his face and emphasize all its nuances.

There was so much that was compelling inside the cool shell he showed to the world, compelling and dynamic and even dangerous. Her chest felt like it was going to burst just looking at him, and again she wondered about the intensity of her feelings, that she was in love with this man who only allowed her bits and pieces of himself.

They stopped at a traffic light, and Steven looked over at her. "My condominium is not far from here." It was both a statement and a question, one that allowed her to ignore the latter if she chose. How could he possibly think that she would?

But she was going to make him say it. She just looked at him quizzically, waiting.

"Would you like a drink?"

She pretended to mull over the idea. "Yep," she said finally.

He looked at her suspiciously. She was usually more enthusiastic in her reactions. He was wondering himself about the invitation. Why had he invited her to the austere, uninviting place he called home? He had already said too much tonight. Did he think, perhaps, that the condominium would turn her off, would show her what he really was? Damn. Something deep inside him wanted her to know him, to know all about him; yet he'd perfected being alone so well, he couldn't force himself to reveal more than he had. Especially after those few cryptic words at the restaurant. Even then, he didn't know where they had sprung from.

"Steven?"

The light turned green, and his foot pressed down the gas. "Change your mind?" His question was abrupt, revealing relief.

"No, I just wanted to tell you how good dinner was tonight."

She moved over, and her hand rested on his leg. Red-hot heat, like a brand, drove through him. He wanted her. He wanted her like he'd never wanted anything in his life. He wanted to touch her, to love her, to feel her in his arms. He wanted to feel whole again, like only she could make him.

The wild, unthinking passion she aroused in him scared him. Any kind of violent emotion in himself scared him. And now he felt twisted around like a pretzel. Everything he had known and believed was falling down around him. Even Cherokee Hills was taking second place to this . . . obsession.

That scared him even more than the other.

He tried to jerk himself back to priorities, priorities that he understood.

"Are we all set for next weekend?"

It took Gillian a moment to understand. *Oh yes, the grand opening.* The reason for them meeting, for being together. In the beginning. Only Steven would think of business at a time like this, at a time every nerve in her body was tingling with expectation and her fingers ached to touch him in a far more intimate way than she could now.

"Of course," she said as lightly as she could. "You have a very efficient agency."

"I used to be an efficient developer," he said dryly, "before I met the other half of my efficient agency."

"Are you complaining, sir?"

His lips twisted in that half grimace, the one he wore when he was obviously trying to fight a smile. "I don't think so."

"Think? That doesn't sound like my usually confident client."

"That's because nothing about us is usual," Steven said.

"I don't think so either," she said happily.

"You're hopeless," he observed.

"My greatest dream is to make you hopeless also," she retorted. "If hopeless means what I think it means."

"And what's that, Gillian?"

"Sort of free and happy," she said, liking the sound of her name on his lips. He seemed to avoid it most of the time, resorting to the formal "Miss Collins," or whatnot.

He was silent as he negotiated a turn and then pulled into a side street. The community was modern, composed mostly of one- or two-story buildings of stucco. There were skylights and lots of windows and well-tailored grounds, and if she'd been asked the type of home he would pick, this would have been it. Practical and attractive but without many frills.

He drove into a carport and turned off the engine. She allowed him to make his way around to her door and open it, and when he held out his hand, she just sort of fell into his body, feeling it tense against her. "God help me," she heard him mutter.

"I think He planned the whole thing," she whispered in reply.

He gave her that arched-eyebrow look again, as if to tell her she was absolutely crazy. Well, she was. About him, anyway. And he was about her too. She knew it. Even if he didn't want to admit it vocally. He did in other ways. Like taking her to dinner tonight. And the way he made love to her last night. And the way he got sort of confused with what he was saying when he looked at her.

That was sufficient for the moment.

So was his taking her hand and holding it tightly as they walked to the front door.

Gillian hadn't known what exactly to expect inside. He was still too much an enigma in so many ways, but she had expected *something*.

Instead, she had the feeling of walking into a model home, a place where no one really lived. There were a few magazines on a glass-and-chrome coffee table, but no other signs of life. Not even a mussed pillow. It was disgusting.

It was also fairly expensive, she realized. She knew enough from Leslie's clients to recognize quality if not homeyness. Steven glanced around, his gaze settling on an answering machine hooked to the telephone. A little red light blinked.

Gillian hated those things. She always had the feeling she was being screened and found wanting when no one answered. It was ridiculous, she knew, but still . . .

Steven pressed the button, and she looked for something to do so as not to look as if she were eavesdropping, no matter how much she wanted to.

But the voice coming out over the machine was not quiet. "Stevie . . . I've got great news. Give me a call and save Wednesday night for me. I promise the world won't blow up if you do. And bring a friend. Of the female persuasion." There was a slight hesitation. "Just come. Please." The last word was oddly pleading compared to the assurance in the rest of the message.

Steven didn't move for a moment, then turned back to her. "My brother," he explained simply.

"Stevie?" Gillian asked the question with a quirky smile, but her eyes were much more serious. And asking another question altogether. Ask me for Wednesday, she begged silently.

He looked at her, his body filling with tension. He wished like hell he hadn't played the message. Not now, when she was so close and he wanted to hold her so badly. Taking her to meet Bobby was a commitment, one he wasn't ready to make, might never be ready to make, considering his past. Still, the message hovered in the air between them, and he reacted as he usually reacted to her, doing just the opposite of what he thought he should do. "Are you free Wednesday?"

"Yes."

"No appointment book to look at?"

"Nope," she said airily, not bothering to add that

if she had something else, she would find a way to break it.

He strode over to her, and leaned down, his lips caressing hers. "I've never met anyone like you."

"I hope not."

She didn't have an ounce of guile in her, he thought as he looked down at her. Her eyes fairly danced with pleasure at his invitation, just as they'd been oddly hesitant only seconds before when he knew she'd heard Bobby's invitation.

What was so damned important? That was the first time Bobby had made a meeting sound imperative. Their previous meetings had always been very casual, sometimes almost by accident. He now wondered why neither had made more effort. But then he knew. Deep down, he knew why. There was too much pain there. Too many memories, and both had tried to forget them, to closet them, and that attempt had driven them apart rather than closer.

He gestured toward a bar in the corner. "What would you like?"

"You."

Her hand had crept up to his chin that was now set with tension. He felt himself relax under her touch, the control slipping as it always did with her. Her smile always lit the space she was in, even the space within him.

In a gesture so spontaneous, it shocked him, he swept her up in his arms and carried her into his bedroom. With each step he was very, very aware of the way she snuggled close to him, her head resting against his heart, her arms around his neck possessively, possessively and trustingly.

Their clothes were discarded in record time and now their lovemaking was frantic, Gillian feeling the storm in him and feeding it. She wanted him that way, full of passion and emotion, the control ripped by the violence and intensity of their components.

He came into her hard and demanding, and her own newly awakened sensuality responded in instinctive ways, moving with him, against him, in wonderful rhythmic dances that built the exquisitely lustful sensations until Gillian thought she could bear no more. And then in one last wonderful thrust, all those breathless, rushing responses exploded in a fireball of glory. She felt him collapse on her, felt his ragged breathing. Then he touched his lips against her cheek almost reverently, and the physical reactions still causing her body to tremble were joined by an emotional joy so strong, she felt tears gathering behind her eyes. There was so much wondering tenderness in that touch.

Whether he realized it yet or not, Gillian knew in that moment that he loved her too. She just didn't know whether or not he would ever admit it.

His lips moved from her cheek to her mouth, and warmth replaced heat; sweetness, violence; and caring, passion.

Gillian felt as though she were wrapped in a big fluffy ball of cotton candy. Safe. Loved. She looked up at his face, the strong face she had grown to love, even grown to understand a little, and it was softer than she'd ever seen it.

"You feel so good there," she whispered.

"You feel so good everywhere," he said. "Too damned good."

"How can anyone feel too good?"

"Damn if I know," he admitted ruefully. He started nibbling on her earlobes. "You taste good too."

"Steven."

"Huhhhhh?" he mumbled, his attention occupied by the nape of her neck.

"Nothing. I just like to say it."

He lifted his head then from where he'd been nibbling and stared at her steadily. "Ah Gillian, no one has ever made me feel this way before."

"How?"

"So . . . I don't know . . . mindless, I suppose."

"I hope I make you feel other things too."

"Oh, you do. How you *do* do that!"

"Tell me."

"You're shameless."

"Completely," she agreed.

"Should I count the ways?"

"Elizabeth Barrett Browning," she said gleefully. "You surprise me, Mr. Morrow."

"All us jocks are illiterate?"

"Oh no," she argued in self-defense. "It's just that you never seem like you have time."

"A few things stick here and there," he said with a slight smile.

"So tell me? How do I make you feel."

"I would rather show than tell," he said with a taunting smile.

"That's cheati—" But the last of the sentence was stopped by his lips. And he did indeed show instead of tell.

Gillian decided she preferred that too.

Sated and content, Gillian nestled in his arms. A glimmer of light shone across Steven's face from a hall fixture. Her fingers went over and caressed the lips that had given her so much pleasure that night. His features wer relaxed, his eyes half closed, and he looked more approachable and vulnerable than in all the hours she'd spent with him.

She snuggled up closer to him. "Tell me about Bobby."

"Robert," he said. "If you called him Bobby, he'd probably glare at you. It's undignified for a soon-to-be partner in a major law firm."

Gillian detected the pride in his voice, and smiled inwardly. "You did."

"I'm his older brother. I can get away with a few things other people can't."

"Tell me about him."

She could feel his shrug, his usual response to questions. "He's very bright."

"Is he like you?"

"What am I like?"

"Wonderful."

There was a silence. His arms tightened around her just a little bit, just enough that she felt the change.

"Now what is *he* like? A workaholic too?"

"He works for a corporate law firm. You have to be a workaholic to do that."

"It runs in the family?"

There was a pause.

"I suppose," he said reluctantly.

"Even when you were young?" she persisted.

"I don't think I was ever young," he said. "Neither was Bobby." There was a wistfulness in his voice she'd never heard before, and she knew suddenly that it was true. She remembered him saying he'd never had a pet, nor been to a circus. What kind of childhood had he had?

Part of her didn't want to know. She didn't think she could stand to know why he still guarded himself so well, why he really didn't know how to laugh.

The other part had to know.

"Why?"

"We were . . . poor. My father was hurt in a mill accident and, back then, you didn't get settlements. My mother . . . was often . . . sick and couldn't work. There were four boys. Four boys eat a lot. At least, they like to eat a lot. So I worked."

"And your brothers?"

"When they were old enough. I was the oldest, then Timothy, Bobby and Mike."

"Where's Timothy?" There was a slight tensing again of his body, and Gillian wondered whether she should stop, but this was the first time he'd ever said much about himself or his family.

"He died in Lebanon. In the bombing of the Marine barracks."

She swallowed a lump in her throat. There was something in the way he said it, something that rang any number of warning bells inside her. And she didn't know why.

"And Mike's the one in California?"

"You remembered."

"I remember everything about you."

There it was, Steven thought. That openness again. The openness that scared the wits out of him.

She wanted to ask more, but for once in her life she held her tongue. She remembered the sharpness with which he had said his mother and father were dead. She tried to steer the conversation to a happier sphere, now that he was, at least, talking.

"And what do you do for enjoyment, when you have a day off?"

Steven looked at her in an odd way, as if he'd never considered such a possibility.

She shook her head. "Don't tell me. I know. Work."

"It's the only way . . ."

She hushed him with a brush of her lips. And then her hand brushed the thick, crisp hair, relishing the feeling, relishing the deepening of the gray in his eyes as she did so. She was astounded at how much she cared, at how much she wanted to make him laugh. A chuckle was a major achievement. A real laugh, now that would be something. Really something. She licked his ear. Funny how good it tasted. She'd never really licked body parts before. But her voice was all seriousness when she spoke. "No, love, it's not. It's a terrible cliché, but sometimes you have to stop and smell the roses. It really does increase your effectiveness afterward."

Teach me. He said the words to her in his mind, but he couldn't vocalize them. It represented an invitation, an invitation to breach the walls he'd built, but then hadn't he done just that when he'd invited her to Bobby's? He hadn't really intended that. But it happened, just like everything just happened with Gillian Collins. It was almost as if she were a witch, he thought again. A beguiling witch. And he was discovering he liked being bewitched.

He stretched out on the bed with a long, sated movement. If not exactly smelling roses, he was getting another version of her suggestion. He found himself reveling in the sensuality of the aftermath of lovemaking, of the feel of her body. It was so soft and even smelled of those very roses. He could get used to her smile, and spontaneous laughter, and the way she tipped her head to challenge him. He could get very used to holding her, and making love to her. Very, very used to it.

She wriggled contentedly in his arms, not asking for a reply to her comment about roses, just obviously happy to be exactly where she was. Tenderness curled inside him at the thought. He was giving her a piece of happiness, not just physical pleasure, but deep down happiness, and it was good, so very good. He felt suddenly like he'd caught a butterfly in his hands, and it was content to remain there, not fluttering its wings in anxiety, but trusting as it had not trusted before. That was obvious since she'd been a virgin.

He leaned down over her, feeling like a king both for her gift of giving, and his own. His lips brushed hers as lightly as if she were that butterfly, and could be bruised as easily.

"I have my own rose here," he said quietly, meaning it.

And he would learn to nurture it. As soon as the grand opening was over, as soon as the success of Cherokee Hills was assured. Time. Just a little time.

His arms tightened around her and once more their lips met, and the vise around his heart loosened.

It wasn't until seven the next morning that reality set in.

Sunday. It was Sunday, and light streamed through the windows of his bedroom.

Gillian's arms were still around him, and when she lazily opened her eyes she found him looking at her.

"You're beautiful in the morning."

She gave him an entrancing smile, her large brown eyes partially closed and her lips swollen from kisses during the night. "No one's beautiful in the morning."

"I didn't think so either, but I've found the exception to the rule." The words came out a little stuffily, but Gillian had learned to love that side of him, the slightly uncomfortable side that took refuge in clichés. But then she had been guilty of her own this past night. Perhaps they both were hiding behind them.

"I think you must be prejudiced." Gillian hoped so.

"Maybe. I'm also very observant."

"One of a number of talents, Mr. Morrow."

He nuzzled her. "Would you like to elaborate?"

"I don't think I need to," she said as she stretched like a contented cat. "But I have to go home. My critters." The last was said with wistful resolve.

"And I have to get some work done. You've shot my schedule to hell and back."

"Hmmmm, I like that idea," she said.

He shook his head with mock dismay. "You're hopeless."

"You've said that before."

"I know," he said ruefully. "You seem to take the greatest pleasure in upsetting my schedule."

"That's what schedules are for," she replied complacently.

"And you never have a schedule?"

She thought about that for a moment. It would be a lie to say she didn't. She had a very definite schedule in her mind, and things always got done. Sometimes at the wire, she admitted only to herself, but they did get done. In many ways, she was as responsible as Leslie, and, as far as she knew, had never let down a client. It just wasn't a, well, rigid thing.

She nibbled on his earlobe before answering. "Maybe, a bit," she admitted. "But some things just kind of pop up and you have to be flexible."

The words were innocently said, but Steven started chuckling. Gillian heard the noise start deep in his throat, and reviewed her comment. Then she started giggling. "I didn't mean that. Exactly."

The chuckle grew louder, and turned into full-fledged chest-deep laughter, and she stared in delight as the skin around his eyes crinkled and the smallest dimple manifested itself on one of his cheeks.

He scooted up on the bed, leaning his body against the headboard as the laughter continued, as if it had been bottled up inside for a long time and was now exploding outward.

Gillian couldn't help but join him, and the mingled sounds of amusement echoed in the room as once more something popped up and they became very flexible indeed.

ELEVEN

Gillian hesitated before entering Steven's outer office. She tried to put on her business face, but she was very much afraid her "I'm in love" face was there instead.

It was Monday, and she had all the final radio copy for the advertising which would start Wednesday and run repeatedly through Saturday.

The full-page ad approved by Steven had run in the Sunday papers. Similar advertisements would run in the weekly papers and in the dailies' Friday editions.

She hadn't seen Steven since she'd arrived home Sunday morning. Twenty-four hours ago. It seemed a lifetime now. And she didn't know what to expect this morning.

Steven had been quiet when he'd left her on the doorstep. The nonsense was gone and some of the usual austerity back in his expression. He'd pecked her lightly at her door, waited until she got inside to find everything in fairly good shape, and then said good-bye.

"I'll see you Monday," he'd said, and Gillian knew he meant at work. But just before turning to leave, he smiled. "Thank you," he said simply, and left.

Thank you for what? She wasn't quite sure. But still, despite his moodiness, she'd felt wonderful all day Sunday. She remembered the song from *My Fair Lady*, or at least snatches of it. The part about feeling happy and giddy and gay and all those good things.

But now, Monday, he would expect professionalism, and he had every right to expect it. But could she really resist touching him? Could she really keep her eyes steady and her hands to herself?

His secretary told her to go in. He was sitting on the corner of the desk, looking harried and impatient, and his eyes softened only a little when he saw her.

"Miss Collins," he acknowledged, and Gillian hated the impersonality of his voice.

"Mr. Morrow," she retorted. "You look . . . well today."

"Strange," he observed. "I haven't slept much. But let's look at those radio ads, and my secretary will give you a check."

Money. Of course. Being a small agency, she and Leslie always asked for the advertising money up front. But money had been the least of her worries during the past few days.

She nodded. "Things are going well at Cherokee Hills?"

"Almost finished," he said with satisfaction. "I'm just worried about the weather now. I've been doing a dry dance every night."

The comment was so unexpected that it took Gillian a moment to catch it. And then she grinned, thinking of him in that fastidious apartment doing the opposite of an Indian rain dance. Whatever that was.

"You must be very good at it. I checked with one of the television stations today. No rain in sight . . . anyplace."

"I live a clean life."

Once again his deadpan tone nearly threw her. He kept surprising her that way. "You don't have time to do anything else," she observed.

"Touché," Steven said. "And so I don't, right now, but I'll see you Wednesday night. Is eight okay?"

Gillian felt a stab of disappointment at the almost curt dismissal and also the fact that she would have to wait until Wednesday, but she understood. Not only understood, but should be grateful. She knew him now, knew how much he suppressed under that stern mask of his, and she had a load of work of her own to do. "Sounds great."

He hesitated a moment, then rose, accompanying her to the door. "I meant it yesterday," he said softly. "Thank you."

"You're very welcome, Mr. Morrow," she said. "Very, very welcome."

If Gillian hadn't been so busy in the next two days, she would have suffered terribly, both from withdrawal and from doubts. But she didn't have time.

She visited every news editor in town, promoting the Russian circus and the grand opening, twisting arms, calling in every favor, hinting how it might make a good national television bit, since Russia was so much in the news today. Just days earlier, one of the networks had a piece on a Russian sailing ship, recreating the exploration voyage from Russia to the northwest coast, which had also run out of money and was stranded.

That, together with the governor's appearance in the celebrity golf tournament, almost guaranteed substantial media coverage, unless there was some major breaking local story.

Interspersed between those visits was work for her own clients, contact with two of Leslie's clients, and finally a visit to the motel where Sergei and the circus stayed.

Sergei was full of optimism. Costumes were being brightened, performers were practicing, a new sense of hope had infused the complete troupe. There had been local publicity, of course, about their plight, but now the governor would be forced to take notice, along with other dignitaries, perhaps even the whole country.

The only sour note was that all the performers couldn't be included. But Gillian had an idea.

She knew what Steven had ordained, that the circus activities were to be limited to the park areas, but that would make it more difficult for the media, for the television cameras. She was only too aware of the media's limited time and staff over weekends. She also knew how important this opening was to Steven, how important Cherokee Hills was to him, and she believed with all the instinct she so strongly relied upon that the circus was the key to success, to making Cherokee Hills unique and special and welcoming.

There were dozens of Cherokee Hills in Atlanta. Perhaps they didn't have the painstaking care that Steven had given his, but how many people really noticed those small quality details? Perception. That was the key.

But she knew she couldn't tell Steven what she thought. He had already given more than she'd expected, and she knew him well enough now to know he wouldn't yield further. He was stubborn.

Almost as stubborn as she was.

Gillian pulled Sergei aside and together they plotted.

Gillian eyed her wardrobe carefully. She would be meeting Steven's brother. An attorney. Should she be more conservative? No, she finally decided. She had to be herself.

He had to like her for herself. Just as she was learning to love Steven for himself.

She finally selected a black jersey blouse, and a long red skirt trimmed with black braid. She clasped her waist with the silver belt, and softened the severe neck of her blouse with a bright red scarf which accented her dark hair. She brushed her hair until it shone and then made a French braid. She finished with the large silver hoop earrings she usually wore.

She looked a little like a gypsy, she knew, but it seemed to suit her. It certainly would be a contrast to Steven's usual conservative appearance. What was his brother like? Grave, like Steven? Conservative, like Steven?

Gillian had never been really nervous about meeting anyone before. She usually didn't know what a stranger was. Now, uniquely, her stomach felt like a mixer. With this invitation, even if it were a trifle reluctant, Steven had invited her into his life, and she suspected he didn't do that often. She desperately didn't want to disappoint him.

She put on some lipstick and the least bit of mascara, and took Spenser out, returning and pacing back and forth in the small living area.

Steven was right on time, just as she knew he would be, and looked gorgeous. He looked more gorgeous each time she saw him, but now he seemed even more so. Instead of the usual suit, he wore a smoky-blue cable-knit sweater and dark blue slacks. He looked relaxed, although small lines of what seemed to be weariness, or strain, snaked from the edges of his eyes.

"Hi," he said simply, his arms at his side, and Gillian sensed the awkwardness in him, awkwardness she knew was unusual.

But she didn't feel awkward. She stretched upward

and kissed him, her lips savoring the remembered taste of him, and his own mouth responded, deepening the kiss while he wrapped her in his arms. "God, I missed you," he groaned when he finally released her lips, and Gillian knew it was not an altogether voluntary statement.

"Me too," she said.

He just looked at her, as if he couldn't get enough. "You look lovely."

"Not too much like a gypsy?"

"A beautiful gypsy. I'm going to have to warn my brother to keep hands off."

No need, she thought. Steven had blinded her to everyone, everything else.

"Should we go, or would you like something to drink first?"

Steven was afraid what might happen if he were alone with her in that cottage. "We'd better go," he said, swallowing the raw want that had seized him when he saw her.

She nodded. She picked up her purse and joined him at the door, watching him lounge against the wall with deceptive ease.

He took her hand and escorted her to the pickup truck and helped her inside. They were on their way.

Steven felt a tightening of his gut. He still didn't know what Bobby wanted. It couldn't be anything bad or his brother would not have asked him to bring a date. He had called but had received precious little information.

Just an informal dinner at his home, Robert had said. Home was a restored Victorian cottage in one of Atlanta's in-town communities, just two blocks from Robert's office. His brother had made a real home out of it, with warm, inviting furniture. There were scattered photographs of Steven in his University of Georgia football uniform, photographs of their brother, Mike, and his family, a rare photograph of the three of them.

And Steven looked forward to the meal. Robert was a damned good cook. All of the brothers had learned to be; it was the only way they ate.

Steven felt Gillian's gaze on him, and it started all his senses tingling. He still couldn't believe how glad he'd been to see her, how pure joy surged through him at the twinkling in her dark eyes. He realized he'd just plowed through the last three days, not really alive at all but just going through motions. Cherokee Hills, which had once excited him so much, still did, of course, but now he'd found something that had been missing, the jigsaw puzzle piece that made him whole.

As he drove toward Robert's home, he stole a glance at her. "How has your week gone?" It was not what he wanted to say at all. But, as so often with her, his thoughts didn't translate to speech but stuck someplace between his mind and his mouth. Years of protectionism.

"Busy." It wasn't at all what she wanted to say. But

she was afraid to say anything else, afraid she'd send him deeper into hiding.

"Me too."

Gillian cringed a little at the mundane conversation, particularly after the others they'd had. She hated herself for hiding. It wasn't like her at all. She usually met everything headlong, just as she'd told Leslie to do. But then she'd never been in love before.

She wasn't sure she liked it, the changes it was making in her, the caution.

"This is ridiculous," she said suddenly.

He turned toward her, the left eyebrow raising again.

"Tiptoeing around everything," she explained though she didn't think he needed an explanation.

"Is that what we're doing?"

Gillian suddenly wanted to hit him.

"Steven," she said in a warning voice.

"I know," he finally said, a measure of frustration in his voice. "At least I used to think I knew."

"Ah, admitting some uncertainty?"

"Am I that bad?"

"No, you're really quite wonderful."

"I don't think anyone ever thought that before."

"Then you didn't read your newspaper clippings when you played football."

The car suddenly jerked forward with a burst of speed. "*You* read them."

"I like to know everything about a client," she said airily although she knew it sounded like the lie it was.

"And what did you learn?" His voice was suddenly hostile.

"That you were very good, that an accident stopped a pro career."

There was a sign. "That was a long time ago."

"There has to be something comforting about being the best at what you do."

"Comforting? That isn't the word I would use."

"Not even now? Looking back? Just knowing how good you were?"

"I don't look back, Gillian. And even if I did, there's nothing in the world more useless than a broken football player. He's unique that way."

She searched for bitterness in the words, but there wasn't any. Merely a statement of fact. She ventured a little further. "I imagine there were a lot of . . . girls attracted to a star player."

His jaw set, and Gillian instantly regretted the question, but he answered. "Like I said, there's nothing more useless than an injured football player." This time, there was bitterness in the words and something of the ease between them dissipated.

Gillian bit her lip to keep from responding, and they rode the rest of the way in silence.

But when they stopped in front of a charming Victorian house with a yard full of trees and rosebushes, he helped her from the truck and his hand clasped hers with the earlier warmth.

The house was so completely different from Steven's condominium that Gillian had a difficult time accepting the fact it belonged to his brother.

Just then the door opened, and a man appeared, and again Gillian had to rearrange her thinking. Where Steven was tall and powerful in build, his brother was middle height and looked more like a teddy bear than a tiger. While not fat or probably even overweight, he gave an impression of . . . cuddly. His hair was light brown, instead of sandy like Steven's, and his smile easy. But the eyes, a piercing light blue, reflected a sharp, probing intelligence as they studied her for the briefest of seconds and then turned warm. It was a remarkable transformation.

He offered his hand to Steven and gave him a bear hug which surprised Gillian for some reason, and then he turned to Gillian. "I'm Robert," he said. "And Steven didn't tell me what a beautiful woman he was bringing."

Gillian, who had never been shy, found herself blushing. She liked Robert on sight. She liked the way he'd greeted Steven and she liked that brief moment of inspection that hinted of protection.

"This is Gillian," Steven said. "Gillian Collins. She's the advertising genius behind Cherokee Hills."

"I saw the ad this week," Robert said, "and heard the radio spots. They're good. But I don't envy you working for my brother."

Gillian grinned at him. "We've had our battles."

Robert eyed her again, this time a little more carefully, and Gillian felt a sudden warmth when he smiled with approval. "Perhaps Stevie's found his match."

Steven glared at him, and Gillian wasn't sure

whether it was because of "Stevie," or the implication of the words.

"Let's go inside, *Bobby,*" he said, a warning in his voice.

Robert grinned at Gillian. "Loosens him up every time," he said facetiously.

"Typical attorney's misjudgment," Steven retorted, but Robert merely smiled before turning and leading the way in.

Another woman was standing just inside, as if waiting for them to enter, and Robert went over to her, winding his arm around her waist. "My news," he said with great formality and even a bit of awe. "This is Jeannie, and last week she agreed to marry me."

There was a sudden pause in the room, almost as if the air had been sucked from it. Despite a certain emotion in his voice, Robert's face was almost expressionless now, watchful, the way Gillian supposed he might be in a courtroom, and she saw, more clearly now than since she first met Robert, the resemblance between brothers. Robert shared that odd wariness, that ability to hide feelings; but he hid behind affability where Steven hid behind austerity.

Surprise had momentarily ripped the mask from Steven's face, and then it softened in a way that made Gillian's heart pound. "I'm happy for you, Robert, and you, Jeannie," he said, sincerity obvious in his voice. "Congratulations."

Gillian was fascinated at the interchange. Something was hanging unsaid in the air.

"I was going to wait to tell you at dinner," Robert said, "but . . ." He shrugged. "Isn't she beautiful?"

Gillian's and Steven's gazes both went to Jeannie who herself was blushing now. She wasn't beautiful, not in the accepted way. Her face was a little plump, but it was softened by short light brown, almost golden hair that feathered around her cheeks. The most striking impression was the just plain niceness of her face; you knew instantly you would like this person because of the smile and the soft warmth in her eyes. They were a deep shining green whose gaze told everyone she obviously adored Robert.

Gillian had to smile at the look the two exchanged. She wondered if she looked at Steven that way. She turned her head to look at him, but his attention was focused on his brother and sister-in-law-to-be with a bemused expression on his face. She would have given everything she had, except Spenser and No Name, to know what he was thinking.

"If you'd warned me," Steven said, "I would have brought champagne."

"Already done, brother mine," Robert said and reluctantly let go of Jeannie to disappear into another room.

Steven was still looking after his brother in a rather strange way, and suddenly he followed Robert. "I'll help."

Gillian turned her gaze toward Jeannie. "When is the wedding?"

"Next month sometime," Jeannie said, her face shining. "The exact date is up in the air. Robert wants

Steven to be his best man, so it depends on when he's available."

Gillian instinctively went over and hugged her. "You look so happy."

"I am," she said softly so the men couldn't hear. "I don't think commitments come easily in this family." And then she looked startled as if she was surprised at her own words.

Gillian knew exactly what she meant, but she didn't have time for more conversation because the two men were coming back into the room, Robert holding a bottle of champagne and Steven four glasses.

Robert grinned at Jeannie. "He agreed. Anytime after Steve's opening. You set the date."

The cork was popped, and a glass of champagne placed in Gillian's hand. Steven made the toast, a very simple one. "To happiness."

Gillian heard an odd, wistful note in his voice, as if he really didn't think happiness existed but hoped for his brother's sake it did. She moved over to him, and put her empty hand in his and he looked down at her with a soft twist to his lips that made her heart spin.

But the conversation turned to the upcoming wedding. Jeannie, she discovered was a legal secretary at the law firm where Robert worked, and she wanted only a small wedding at the church she and Robert attended.

At the last statement, Steven's eyebrow went up in his brother's direction, and Robert shrugged with a kind of resigned grin.

Dinner followed. It was apparently a joint effort between Robert and Jeannie, and included stuffed mushrooms and veal Parmesan with a wonderful Italian salad. Steven was quiet, as he often was, but was obviously absorbing everything, every glance between his brother and Jeannie, every word, as if weighing them. Robert kept the conversation going, asking Gillian about herself, about her business, although his eyes kept turning toward Jeannie with a warmth Gillian envied.

"How's the opening coming?" Robert finally asked Steven, his own gaze moving between his brother and Gillian.

"Pretty much on target," Steven said.

"The circus sounds like a great idea."

"The credit goes to Gillian," Steven said. "She convinced me."

"Well, it's brilliant. You couldn't get me out there with a golf tournament, but Jeannie wants to see the circus."

"Et tu, Brutus," Steven said, but there was a grin on his face. "You aren't thinking about buying in Cherokee Hills? I thought you loved this house."

"I do, but . . . we'll be looking for a larger place."

"With all pride aside, you can't do better than Cherokee Hills."

"I know," Robert said. "You never do anything halfway." He hesitated. "Which is why I don't see nearly enough of you. I'm glad you and Gillian came tonight."

"My little brother doesn't get engaged every day."

"Not so little anymore." He looked over at Gillian. "He put both my brother and me through college . . . and me through law school," he said.

Steven looked decidedly uncomfortable. "You did it yourselves."

"Not without your financial help. I don't know whether I told you how damned grateful I am. I know how much you hated that damned job."

Something, a look, passed between the two brothers that puzzled Gillian. But then Steven had puzzled her since that first dinner they'd shared. She'd never seen so many layers on a person; whenever she peeled back one, she'd find ten more.

Gillian offered to help with the dishes, and Robert chimed in. "Why don't Gillian and I do them while Steve and Jeannie get to know each other better?"

Both Steven and Jeannie looked startled and ready to say no, but Gillian jumped up and grabbed some plates. "I think that's a wonderful idea."

Steven couldn't say no without appearing rude to his future sister-in-law. He had been neatly trapped, and Gillian exchanged a conspiratorial look with Robert, who winked.

Gillian and Robert worked efficiently together, Gillian rinsing and Robert putting dishes in the dishwasher. Gillian wanted to ask a million questions but she didn't know how. She found herself unusually shy.

It was Robert who spoke first. "You like Steven, don't you?"

She nodded, and then added with that frankness

she could never quite control. "But I don't really feel I know him."

"Sometimes I wonder if anyone does," Robert said. "But I've never seen him look at a woman the way he looks at you."

"Do you see him much?"

"No. Not as much as I would like. He has a tendency to get completely wrapped up in a project, and nothing else exists for him."

"It's more than that, isn't it?"

Robert's hands stilled. "Don't let him down, Gillian. Too many people have done that."

"Robert . . ."

"He's never said anything about growing up, has he?"

"No."

Robert hesitated. "We had a hell of a life, Steven more than the rest of us because he always took the brunt of it. I think we all developed steel hides. It wasn't until Jeannie . . ." Robert paused and then continued, "I hope you're *his* Jeannie."

"Can you tell me more?"

"No," he said. "He needs to do it. When he's ready. But I can tell you this, he's one hell of a person. He has more strength than anyone I know."

"I know," she said.

Robert looked at her for a long time. "Good. He needs someone."

They heard the door open then, and the sound of voices nearing, Jeannie's laugh and Steven's measured tone. Gillian pondered over Robert's words. *Don't let him down. Too many people have done that.*

She looked at Steven's face and saw his eyes gleam as they settled on her.

No, she would never let him down.

TWELVE

"You didn't expect that, did you?" Gillian posed the question as they drove back to her cottage.

"Expect what?"

"That your brother was getting engaged."

Steven's hands tightened on the steering wheel. "He once swore he would always be a bachelor."

"And you?"

"Me what?"

"Steven!" she said, exasperated.

But he had obviously said all he was going to. He took her hand and pulled her as close to him as he could with the gear shift between them.

He drove the rest of the way in silence, Gillian aching from his touch, from the need to get more from him. More physically. More emotionally.

To her surprise, he hesitated after she'd opened her front door and leaned over to greet a happily pulsating Spenser.

"Will you come in?"

He nodded, his eyes hooded, but once inside he leaned over and kissed her. Hard and sweet. Savage and gentle. All at once, and Gillian felt herself trembling from all the responses inside her.

Her arms went around his neck, and she pressed her body next to his, wanting to meld with him, wanting to melt that reserve that had been with him all evening.

"What you do to me, lady," he said.

"Good," Gillian said, "because you do exactly the same to me."

He folded her in his arms, holding tight, as if pressing a memory into consciousness, as if she might slip away. This sudden tentativeness was so out of character. He was usually so sure, so strong, so positive. She wondered how she could possibly love anyone more than she did Steven at this moment. Would it grow even stronger? Could it?

She tipped her head up and reached on her tiptoes to meet his mouth. She usually liked his height, but not now. She needed his help, and she wasn't sure he was going to give it.

But with a slight groan, he did, and their lips met again and this time he didn't let go, but picked her up and carried her into the bedroom.

They didn't bother to turn on the lights, but hurriedly undressed each other as if their lives depended on speed, as if the other would disappear unless they held on to each other, and they did. He took something from a pocket and turned slightly, and then was back with her. Their fingers wrapped together as they lay down on the bed, and his tongue trailed down her face to the most sensitive part of her earlobe and then to the nape of her neck.

Gillian felt him grow rigid, and her insides burned for him, the pressure growing until she thought she would explode for need of him.

"I want you," she whispered. "I want you so badly. I want you to be part of me, to dance and love inside me." Her body moved against his, tempting and seducing.

"Gillian," he rasped in a hoarse whisper as he lifted up over her and his own body joined in a mating dance. The want, the raw, ragged desire that was pure exquisite pain burgeoned into something close to agony. And then he entered, slowly, teasing as he went, building the pressure in both of them until her body was acting of its own accord, meeting him thrust for thrust, her hands digging into his back, their movements becoming frenetic as he reached into the very core of her. His thrusts slowed, became maddeningly seductive until Gillian felt every nerve end sizzle, every muscle tighten with need and expectation.

"Gillian," he said in a burst of sound, and then the liquid heat inside her exploded, ignited by the friction within them and flamed by roiling emotions. Waves of pleasure followed the heat, surge upon surge of sensations which flooded Gillian's body as Steven collapsed upon her, his manhood still reacting inside and sending new tremors of satisfaction washing through her.

"How could anything be so wonderful?" she said.

He rolled over on his side, taking his weight off

her, but keeping her with him. "I don't know," he whispered. "I never . . ."

His face was damp, and Gillian's lips caressed his skin, tasting the drops of sweat that made it salty. She wanted to say she loved him, and it took all the discipline she'd ever had not to do so. She didn't know whether he was ready to hear it, or whether he would run from those words.

But if she couldn't say those things in words, she knew she was saying them with her lips. And if he couldn't accept words, he was responding to their alternative, his own mouth loving hers with that gentleness that so often counterpointed that curt exterior.

His hands ran up and down the length of her midsection, pausing here and there as an explorer might hesitate at a particularly interesting terrain, and then move on. It was a loving, possessive act, and she tingled all over with fiery reaction. His slightest touch was like a brand to dry kindling, his lips an invitation to explode into flames. She felt her body tremble as the need built again. How could it reignite so quickly?

She nuzzled his neck, making wet designs, feeling him grow taut again. She felt her breasts grow taut, too, and she felt his hands on them, and need turned into mindless, naked lust. And pleasure.

So much pleasure.

He stayed the night. Gillian woke periodically and, feeling him against her, closed her eyes in perfect contentment. She woke to a kiss, and he was dressed, sitting beside her. She looked at the clock and groaned. Six A.M.

"I have to go," he said, "but after the opening, we'll talk."

Still sleepily sluggish, she nodded.

"I let Spenser out and fed that other ravenous beast of yours."

"I'm pretty ravenous myself." She grinned lazily, making it very clear she wasn't ravenous for the same reward as No Name.

He smiled. It was a lovely smile. One she hadn't seen before. Sensuous and promising. Open.

She loved it.

He leaned down and kissed her. "Just a few more days, love," he said, and strode to the door, leaving Gillian to luxuriate in the bed that still had his scent and to wonder if he was aware of the last word he'd said.

Steven felt great. He felt better than he'd ever remembered feeling.

Free, even. Free of the past, of the fear that had haunted him. Both Mike and now Bobby had overcome it, and he could, too, the fear that violence ran like a disease in their family.

He'd known it when he'd felt so much tenderness. He'd known then that he, like his two remaining brothers, had escaped the taint of at least two generations of Morrows.

Lord, but he loved Gillian, loved the way she gave so openly, the way she looked at him, the way she responded so readily to his every touch. And he could admit it.

Once Cherokee Hills was well launched, they would have time to explore those feelings, to talk, to share. Share. That was a new word. But one with promise.

He shifted gears, turned at the light, and headed toward Cherokee Hills. He had still another, more vital reason now, for wanting its success.

Gillian only saw Steven briefly in his office Friday to go over final details. He was all business, but his eyes were warm, warmer than ever before except while they were making love, and that image made all the blood rush to her face. But she also saw his distraction, his absorption now with the million details of the opening, and she kept her hands to herself, as difficult as that was.

But she, too, had little time to play. She had been completely occupied with the news media on Thursday, answering questions, setting up blocks of time for television coverage. She talked to the caterers and added two cotton candy machines and a popcorn booth to fit the circus theme.

She spent Friday with Sergei. They and some of the performers took the motel van and drove out to Cherokee Hills and planned exactly what they would do and how to do it. Gillian looked for Steven; she wanted to tell him that their plans had expanded a little, and that they had dropped a surprise into the golf tournament. Perhaps it was just as well, though, that she didn't see him, she told herself. He couldn't say no, and she knew this new plan was going to work.

Sergei was beside himself with optimism, sure that this exposure to the governor and to so many business and political leaders would help them find a way back home. Alexei and his chimp both wore wide smiles, and there was nothing wider than a chimp smile. Gillian had to grin back, quieting the apprehension that had been building inside her.

This had to work for Steven. It had to.

The calls from the media proved the merit of the idea. Instead of limited news coverage of a staid but celebrity-gilded golf tournament, every television and news service now planned to attend. Gillian had planted little seeds everywhere to enlarge the coverage, suggesting that this media source ask the governor whether he planned to help the circus, and that one ask circus members whether they'd ever seen anything like Cherokee Hills, a kind of feature on Russian life. To each one, she gave a different angle, hoping it would excite their interest.

Cherokee Hills would achieve the widest kind of exposure, and, she believed, exactly the right kind: A family community that cares. In all her news releases, she emphasized that funds from the tournament—fees paid by many of the participants who wished to hobnob with the governor, sports and media figures—would go to the children's hospital, and that contributions would be accepted to help the Stars of Russia Circus return home.

She liked that. A community that cared. It was going to work. Cherokee Hills would be a great success. She felt it in her very reliable bones.

Leslie called Friday night. Gillian heard the happiness in her voice, and now she knew exactly how her partner felt. She remembered Leslie's confusion after she met Connor MacLaren, her folksinger, and Gillian also understood that now.

Leslie asked about the opening, and Gillian, full of excited enthusiasm, told her about the changes in the plans, the addition of the circus acts. Leslie's surprise reflected in a brief silence before asking, "Steven agreed?"

Gillian paused. Steven had agreed, perhaps not to everything, but to the concept. "Yep."

"It sounds like a wonderful idea. You must be getting along." There was a sort of hesitancy in the question, and now Gillian understood why her partner hadn't called before. Leslie, responsible, reliable Leslie, had been afraid to.

"Very well," she said smugly.

Her voice must have conveyed more than she'd intended because she heard Leslie's chuckle in the background. "Not you too?"

"I'm afraid so."

"With Steven Morrow?" There was a bit of wonder in the question.

"Uh-huh."

"The same Steven Morrow I know?"

"I think so." Gillian grinned into the phone, the smile in her voice. "He's really quite . . . interesting."

"I thought you said he was dull and pompous and . . ."

"I was wrong."

"Did I really hear Gillian Collins say that?"

"Yep," Gillian said happily.

"And Steven feels the same way?"

"I think so."

"Hmmmmm," Leslie said.

"And how is Connor?"

"As wonderful as ever. That's really why I called. We're coming back, well, *I'm* coming back next week, so I can plan our wedding."

"That's great. When's the grand affair?"

"Two weeks from tomorrow."

"You don't waste time," Gillian said with delight.

"I . . . we don't think it's really very wise for Robin's mother to be traipsing around the country, living in . . ."

"Don't say it. Not the way you and Connor feel about each other."

There was a slight pause. "Will you be my maid of honor?"

"What about Robin?" Gillian posed the question about Leslie's seventeen-year-old daughter.

"She wants to give me away."

Gillian laughed. "I like that."

"So does she." Leslie chuckled.

"She's happy then about the marriage."

"She's happy about the idea of Scotland and men in kilts."

"From my meeting with Connor, I agree."

"Steven does pretty well in a suit."

"I can't deny that," Gillian said. "He looks even better without one."

There was another silence over the phone. "Another wedding in the offing?"

Gillian sighed. "He's elusive."

"That's a good word for him, but knowing you he doesn't have a chance. Remember what you told me about Connor. I should take him and lock him up in a cabin in the woods. Good advice for the gander."

"I'm not quite sure that would work with him," Gillian said. "But I would be delighted to be your maid of honor, and I'll call Robin. She might enjoy the opening tomorrow, since the circus will be there."

"Wonderful. You have the number, of course."

"Yep, I've already called several times, and we went out to dinner."

"Thanks, Gilly."

"I miss you, Leslie." Gillian's voice was suddenly serious.

"I know, Gilly. I miss you, too, but I also feel . . . wonderful."

"Mmmmmm," Gillian murmured. "Me too. Strange, isn't it?"

"Strange and frightening and . . . splendid."

"I like that word."

"Good night, Gillian."

"G'night."

Gillian called Robin and made arrangements to pick her up at eight the next morning for the opening. She listened to Robin's bubbling excitement about the wedding, and wondered whatever happened to her young friend's initial skepticism about her mother's marriage. But Connor MacLaren had worked his charm on the daughter as well as the mother, and Robin was more excited than Gillian ever remembered her.

Robin had always been special to Gillian, and Gillian had meant to see her more while Leslie was out of town. But Steven had pushed nearly everything from her mind. So she was pleased now when Robin accepted her invitation to the opening to see the circus.

"Bring your sketching pad," Gillian said. "There'll be some great scenes. A mime you'll love. Horses. A chimp. I can probably even put you to work if you want."

"Ugh," Robin said. "I'd rather sketch."

"Anything your heart desires. See you tomorrow."

"Right. Thanks, Aunt Gilly," Robin said.

And it was a good night. As Gillian got into bed and climbed between the sheets, she remembered the feel of Steven there, and what he'd said Thursday morning. After the opening . . . after the opening . . . after the opening . . .

After the opening . . .

THIRTEEN

As she slowly approached the outskirts of Cherokee Hills, Gillian knew the opening was drawing a larger than expected crowd.

Steven had hired several off-duty policemen, even before they had added the circus. He had thought that stars from the Atlanta football, baseball, and basketball teams would be big draws.

But whether the main attraction was the sports figures or circus, people were coming. Traffic had slowed to a crawl and even at this early hour it seemed every spare inch along the streets was filled with parked cars. She showed a special pass and was allowed through to the country club building. Banners and bright-colored flags gave the entire development a festive look, and when she stopped the car she heard the omph pah of the circus band someplace. Robin, who had been regaling Gillian with phone conversations with her mother over the past few days, grinned.

"I think I see your touch, Aunt Gilly," which was the honorary title she'd been given by Robin.

Gillian parked in one of the few reserved places, and her gaze immediately sought out Steven. Instead, she saw Sergei's troupe everywhere, even places it shouldn't be.

Some jugglers had taken over the tennis courts; the mime was greeting everyone and drawing a huge audience. Barking indicated that the dogs were nearby.

Laughter came from down where the golf pro shop sat, and Gillian followed the sound. Alexei, dressed in his clown's costume, and accompanied by his chimp, was preparing to tee off. Alexei, in any number of gestures, was showing the chimp what to do while the president of a major airline stood back, awaiting his turn, with a bemused look on his face.

Gillian and Sergei had interspersed circus clowns throughout the golf tournament and, as she watched the grinning faces, Gillian knew it was working.

She left Robin and moved away from the golf course, still looking for Steven. The country club staff was catering the opening, all except her last addition of the cotton candy, snow balls, and popcorn, and she had little to do now until the press started to arrive. One radio station, however, was broadcasting right from the event, and she stopped to make sure they had everything they needed.

After a few words, she continued on, finding her way to the park where she knew she would find the horses and the Cossacks, and possibly Steven. She knew he had been fascinated with them.

Dmitri, the leader of the group, was busy taking the animals from horse trailers, and they were obviously skittish, probably, she thought, from being stabled for so long without their usual exercise and attention.

But there was no Steven.

She watched for a while. A small ring had been established, and Dmitri and the other three members of his troupe were soothing the horses, putting on the colorful bridles and other regalia.

"Is everything all right?" Gillian eyed the horses nervously.

Dmitri had less English than Sergei, but he understood. He nodded eagerly. "Need exercise. High . . . spirits. Be fine."

She turned back to the clubhouse. Jeff Lewis, manager of the club, might know. He was busy outside, supervising the placement of refreshment tables in a roped-off area for participants in the golf tournament. He smiled as he saw her.

"I'm looking for Mr. Morrow," she said.

"Playing with the governor," Jeff said. "They led off this morning."

"Steven's playing golf?" He'd said nothing about it, nor had he ever said anything about playing golf. She realized how little she knew about him, how little he said. But then lately, their minds had been on another form of athletic activity. Still, she felt an unexpected emptiness at the reminder of how little he shared with her. She tried to think back, over their conversations, and now she remembered that she'd asked him to be available at noon for interviews. Nothing more had been said.

Jeff looked at her. "He's a good player, could even be great if he played more, but then Mr. Morrow is good at anything he does."

"I suppose he is," she mumbled in return. Except sharing. She thought about what she knew of him, and it was frustratingly minuscule.

Gillian thanked him and left to follow the crowds that were trailing the golfers, hoping to see Steven. She noted the large clumps of spectators, and realized that he had been right about the tournament draw, but she had also been right. As the Russian clowns went through, there was laughter and delight, and children stayed with the fathers and mothers, giggling happily.

The community was becoming increasingly crowded, and Gillian felt the usual satisfaction at a plan well executed, but there was still a sick feeling in her stomach, a feeling that something was not quite right. She wasn't quite sure whether it was that sudden realization that she knew so little about Steven, or something else.

Just then, a reporter caught her, and she found Sergei for him. The circus performers were everywhere, their costumes like magnets. Even she had not realized how overwhelming it would be, when she and Sergei decided to expand the number of acts and participants, and she wondered about Steven's reaction. She looked at her watch again. It was 11:30 A.M., near the time she'd suggested to the television stations. Already, she watched one television truck make a slow path toward the clubhouse.

She looked down at the slope of the golf course and saw Alexei and Romeo the chimp at one of the greens, and at the same time saw Steven approach the clubhouse with the governor. His jaw tightened as his gaze followed Alexei and the clown's antics, and the sinking feeling in Gillian's stomach deepened. Perhaps she should not have inserted the clowns without his approval. The governor grinned and said something, and Steven flashed a brilliant smile, but Gillian saw the tense set of his shoulders and knew he wasn't happy.

Another television truck arrived, and Gillian hurried over to it, pointing out the various sites where performances were going on, emphasizing the Cossacks. The truck disappeared in that direction, and Gillian gave a sigh of relief. She wanted to talk to Steven before the reporters got to him.

She moved toward him, and Steven turned to face her, his eyes hooded. "Governor, this is Gillian Collins, our public relations counsel. She's the one who arranged for the circus to be here."

But before either she or the governor could say anything, there were shouts, a scream, then more shouts, and everyone seemed to be running. Four white horses, their manes braided with brightly colored ribbons, were galloping toward the crowd which was scattering like seeds. People scooted beneath tables, behind trees, anything they could find.

Women screamed, gathering children and running as the horses veered away from a shouting Cossack running behind them. The governor pushed a woman and her son out of the path of one of the horses and just barely managed to roll away from its hooves.

Steven grabbed a startled child, who was staring wide-eyed at the terrified and confused horses running first one way, then another, and made for the shelter of an oak tree, while Gillian shepherded another group up on the porch of the clubhouse. One of the spooked horses brushed the side of a table, and it turned over, punch and edibles spilling over onto the ground as another table was pulled over by a waiter seeking to escape the path of the horses.

In a second the animals were gone, tearing over the golf course as tournament players ran for safety. Horrified, Gillian looked out from the porch. One of the Cossacks had finally caught the bridle of one of the spooked horses and swung up on the running horse in a spectacular feat of horsemanship. He was now chasing the other three horses, shouting what sounded to Gillian like Russian curses, as jugglers and clowns and other performers joined in the chase. Romeo the chimp followed Alexei, while circus dogs, gaily adorned with hats and neck ruffles, followed the chase, barking as they played what they must have thought was a merry game.

She watched as people slowly emerged from behind turned tables and trees and the clubhouse while television cameras continued to capture all the chaos. Visitors from other parts of Cherokee Hills had evidently heard the shouts and screams and were pouring toward the clubhouse and within full sight of the ruins.

Tournament players were coming up from the course, no longer able to play with the rampaging horses dodging their would-be captors. Food was all over the ground. One of the snow ball machines had been turned over in the scramble, and syrup was seeping down a newly mowed hill to a manicured green like lava from a volcano, leaving a trail that looked like blood.

Gillian knew a disaster when she saw one, and this ranked high on the scale. For Cherokee Hills. For Steven. Her stomach roiling and her heart aching, Gillian looked toward Steven, who was calming the little girl he'd picked up. But though his voice was soothing, his eyes, when they looked up at Gillian, were like the coldest frost she'd ever seen.

It was late afternoon before order was restored, and Gillian realized the full repercussions of the debacle. The realty companies, which listed the homes of the various builders, had names of prospective buyers, but little else since everyone had become distracted by the chaos, the horse chase, the television cameras and their continuous interviews. Cherokee Hills *would* make the news tonight, probably even the world news, Gillian thought. But this was not the kind of news that prompted people to buy. She might well have ruined Steven Morrow today.

The horses, exhausted by the wild rush, had been soothed and placed in the horse trailers. The remainder of the performers, their bright costumes now dull with dust and sweat, had gathered in a corner. Sergei had been effusive with apologies. Apparently, he said, a boy had thrown a rock at one of the horses and, nervous and restless, they had spooked. It had never happened before. The horses were very highly trained. He lifted his hands in a gesture of helplessness and abject regret.

Steven nodded and turned away, from Sergei and from Gillian. The light, which had been shining so bright within his eyes during the past several days, was gone, clouded by that mist of cynicism and practiced indifference Gillian had observed in the beginning.

The crowds dispersed, and the country club staff cleaned up the grounds. Gillian did what she could to help, steering the television reporters to Sergei, who blamed the mishaps on the circus's abandonment and consequent neglect of the animals. The governor made light of the adventure, saying it was the most fun he'd had in years.

But Gillian knew she had let Steven down. He had told her over and over again the kind of image he wanted for Cherokee Hills, and she stubbornly had thought she knew best, and had, without his knowledge, kept upgrading the role of the circus.

It was nightfall before everyone had gone. Robin, who had thought the whole event awesome, had called a friend to get a ride home. She had seen Gillian's preoccupation, had understood that Gilly would stay until the bitter end.

When the last cup had been cleared, and all but a few cars had left the parking lot of the club, Gillian went looking for Steven. It was dusk, and she hadn't seen him in the past few hours. When she finally found him, he was leaning against a tree, almost obscured in the shadows.

"Steven?"

He looked up, his eyes barely visible in the growing darkness. His expression was wary, and only silence followed the sound of his name.

"I'm sorry," Gillian said.

He shrugged, a gesture of defeat that struck through Gillian like a knife. "My fault," he said coolly. "I agreed to everything. *Almost* everything," he amended.

Gillian closed her eyes. It was as if they were a million miles apart. The trust that had been building between them was gone.

"Steven, it wasn't altogether a disaster. The crowds . . ."

"Saw a disaster," he finished for her. "They saw incompetency, irresponsibility. It's just damn good luck no one was hurt." He looked at her, and his voice softened although his expression, that guarded wariness, remained. Closed. Not to be approached. Just as it was in the beginning. Dear God, it hurt. It hurt down to the end of her smallest toe. She felt like her soul was bleeding. "Don't blame yourself," he continued slowly. "It was my doing, and mine alone."

But his attempt to minimize her role did not help. Each word was like a new knife stab into her heart. Whether he meant it or not, it was most certainly *her* incompetency that had caused this. *Her* irresponsibility. All he'd wanted was a nice dignified opening. He didn't have to say the words. She knew in her heart this was all her fault. She was always so sure she was right, she'd steamrollered him into this and then had inserted much more than he'd wanted.

Had she also destroyed his dream?

Don't let him down, his brother had said. *Too many people have done that.*

Perhaps she had let him down more than anyone. And now that aloneness, that solitary barrier he'd raised against the world, was back, and that brief, wonderful "we" was gone. She had the terrible feeling that he regretted opening even a small part of himself to someone, that he would resist relying on anyone again. And that would be the greatest tragedy of all.

"I'm so sorry, Steven," she said, and when he didn't move, she forced her own legs to do so. He obviously didn't want her around, and she didn't blame him. She walked slowly up to the parking lot and stood and watched him as he gazed out over the golf course, the community of which he'd been so proud. He'd pinned so many hopes on this weekend.

Tears glazed her eyes, and a sob choked her throat. Yesterday had been so grand, so full of hope and life. Tonight was nothing but ashes.

FOURTEEN

Gillian didn't know where to turn this time. She knew she usually met life recklessly. She'd never been timid, nor failed to meet a challenge in some way. Rightly or wrongly, she usually attacked it with energy and enthusiasm. Like she had Steven Morrow.

She'd always prided herself on that.

But now she felt very much like being an ostrich. She burrowed deep in the covers of her bed on Sunday, and wished the day would go away. She kept remembering the scene from yesterday, the chaos.

She'd created a disaster for everyone—the circus, Cherokee Hills, Steven . . .

Especially Steven.

She had purposefully avoided the late-night news, and regarded the television set today as she would a ravenous beast waiting to pounce on her, to rerun the worst day in her life.

The phone rang, but she ignored it. She pulled the covers up over her head, and tried to drown the noise out. She thought about escape, but even the moon was too close. Perhaps a black hole in space would do.

And she thought of Steven, always Steven, and the way he had looked last night. Her throat tightened as she remembered him here in bed with her, making love to her in such a wondrous way.

She felt his hands again, his lips nuzzling her ears, her throat, her face; and a horrible emptiness yawned so wide inside, it threatened to swallow her. Spenser apparently sensed her mood and nosed her sympathetically, and No Name jumped up on the bed and nudged under the cover to lick Gillian's face with a sandpaper tongue.

Sunday. Usually, she rose early and went someplace for breakfast while she read the Sunday paper. She shuddered at the thought now. There would be pictures of the opening. She could just see it now: The governor sprawling in the dirt, business executives running for their lives, wreckage every place.

Tears dribbled down her cheeks, and she angrily pushed them away. She had never been one for self-pity.

Still, she was not going to look at a paper this morning.

Gillian finally forced herself from her cocoon of bedcovers and opened the door for Spenser, then dressed in an old sweatshirt and pair of jeans. She needed to think. She needed the consoling healing of nature.

Gillian put out a bowl of milk and cat food for No Name, and called Spenser. They would go up to the mountains today, she and the dachshund. And then Monday maybe she could face the world again.

Maybe.

The phone did not stop ringing. Now Steven knew why he had taken it off the hook last night. When did he put it back on?

Steven looked at the clock and groaned. It was seven in the morning, and he'd gotten precious little sleep the night before. He'd finally taken a hot shower and slugged down a large glass of bourbon, but even that hadn't helped. And this morning it made his mouth feel like cotton, and his head dull and achy.

He wondered where he would go from here. Cherokee Hills would probably survive the fiasco. It was a good development, but now it would take longer, and he didn't know how long he could hold on financially. It was not unlikely that the bank would take over.

But even more painful was the memory of Gillian's face. The self-blame, the regret, the sadness. He had wanted to reach out to her, but he hadn't been able to. He didn't know why. He just couldn't. He had done what he had always done in crises: Drawn inside himself and locked all the doors.

He had meant it when he said he didn't blame her. He had gone into the circus idea with a certain enthusiasm of his own. A once-in-a-million accident had happened, and it wasn't anyone's fault. Still, he couldn't help thinking that, left to his own instincts,

Cherokee Hills would be well on its way to success. His judgment had been clouded by his own desire and need for Gillian, and that was more frightening than even the potential damage to Cherokee Hills. He had lost what he considered so important to his survival: Control of himself.

The phone kept ringing, and finally he reached for the receiver. "Have you seen the paper?" His brother's voice boomed out over the line. "My brother, the hero."

"What in the hell are you talking about?"

"You and the governor. You're all over the papers."

Steven winced, remembering the sight of the governor sprawled over the ground.

There was a chuckle. "I'm sorry I didn't get there. We were going to come today."

Steven groaned.

"Get a paper," Robert said cheerfully and hung up.

Steven slowly rolled out of bed. His mood was anything but good. His project was in shambles, his life was disgustingly empty, and dear God, how he missed Gillian. His body ached from missing her. But the need was so much more than physical. He needed that smile, that bright laughter that dared the world to disappoint her. He needed everything about her.

It was a galling admission.

He reached for the telephone, and then his hand pulled back. He needed to solve some problems first. He couldn't go to her with bankruptcy facing him.

And that brought back the whole Saturday fiasco to his mind.

A paper! He didn't know whether he was up to reading it. Hero? Well, Bobby had a unique way of looking at things.

Steven pulled on a pair of jeans, slipped a sweater over his shoulders and shoved his feet into a pair of Loafers, not bothering with socks. He might as well know the worst. He ran a comb through his hair, but didn't bother to shave.

He looked at the empty bourbon bottle on the table in disgust. He never drank to excess. Never. He remembered his father too well.

He closed his eyes for a moment, recalling those times when his father got hold of liquor, especially that last time. Steven grabbed and held on to the edge of a door, willing that flash of memory away. His mother's scream, the shouts from inside the house. He was coming home from his evening job, and he started running. There was a sound of a body hitting a floor as he opened the door to the small ramshackle house. His father was on the floor, Steven's brother, Tim, over him, his face red with fury, and then . . .

Steven tried to shake the images from his mind. Damn them. Damn. Why couldn't he bury them for good?

He grabbed the keys to his pickup and slammed out of the condominium.

Steven didn't go to pick up a paper. Haunted by memories that now wouldn't let go, by events he had tried to block away for years, he wondered if they weren't a form of post traumatic trauma. Big words for memories. But the flashbacks kept coming.

He found himself driving out to Cherokee Hills, to a lifestyle he suddenly realized he had tried to create for reasons completely separate from those he'd given his investors, his builders, Leslie and Gillian and, subsequently, the press.

He had been trying to reinvent his childhood, to use the development as his own private Disneyland to wipe away those last shadows, to manufacture the perfect place. The circus, the white horses, had added to the mirage. How ironic that they had torn down the fragile house of webs he'd so carefully constructed.

He stopped the pickup short of the development, in the empty parking lot of an office park, almost blinded now by flashbacks. Steven felt emotions surge through him. "You're the strong one," his mother had said. "You have to take care of the others."

But he hadn't been strong, not at seventeen. How breakable he had been, but he couldn't let anyone know it so he'd built a facade. He'd built it so well that the shell had become Steven Morrow, and the real Steven Morrow had disappeared.

Until Gillian.

A cry ripped from his gut, but no one heard it early on a Sunday morning in a vacant parking lot.

❖━━━❖

It wasn't until noon that he finally arrived at Cherokee Hills. He stared at the number of cars parked up and down the tree-lined streets before pulling into the crowded parking lot of the country club, where the sales offices were also located.

There were several copies of the Sunday paper strewn over the comfortable lobby, and he leaned down and picked one up.

"Runaway horses turn community into wild West," said a headline in a featured story at the bottom of the front page. Inserted in the story was a photo of the governor pushing a child out of the way of one of the horses. "Quick action by Governor and developer saves lives." Inside was a photo of Steven holding the little girl he'd grabbed and another of people scattering before the horses.

Attempts to help a Russian circus by a local developer nearly ended in disaster, the story said, *except for quick, efficient action by Governor Ed Davis and developer Steven Morrow.*

The fray apparently started when someone threw a stone at a performing horse. Sergei Chukov, spokesman of the circus, said the animals were high-strung and nervous from lack of exercise while being boarded here.

The circus found itself abandoned by its backers over a month ago in Atlanta and has been unable to get home. Their appearance at the opening of Atlanta's newest residential community was an attempt to raise funds and awareness to help the performers return home to Russia.

The startled horses galloped through the development,

interrupting a celebrity-gilded golf tournament and sending spectators dashing for safety.

Two children in the path of the horses were saved by Governor Davis and Morrow who risked their own lives to push the youngsters out of the way.

One witness, Cecil Notes, said everyone else seemed paralyzed by the quick sequence of events. "I've never seen anything like it. Just like an old western movie. They were real heroes. Gives you a good feeling about this place."

Cherokee Hills is a new concept in residential development in this area. It consists of individual and distinct neighborhoods built around a network of parks, and emphasizes preservation of the natural environment . . .

The story went on, recounting the events of Saturday and the plight of the Stars of Russia Circus. There was a quote by the governor about his rescue, in which he repeated what he'd told Gillian, "It was the most fun I'd had in years." But then he had grown serious and made several statements about the need to help the circus get home. Mr. Morrow had been unavailable for comment.

It was, Steven knew, the greatest publicity in the world, and the number of people prowling the development was proof of it. The realty agents had broad smiles on their faces as they escorted people in and out of offices, and around the clubhouse. Steven heard a few snatches of conversation. "Exactly what we're looking for." "A community that's really a community." "A developer who cares."

Whether Gillian had planned things exactly this way or not, Cherokee Hills was a success.

Steven stayed at Cherokee Hills the rest of the afternoon, speaking to prospective buyers, answering reporters' questions. The story had been picked up by newspapers throughout the country and by network television. He even received a call from the governor. "I can probably be elected President now," he quipped. "Next time you have a grand opening, call me."

Steven knew that the Russian circus was probably receiving similar attention. He tried to call Gillian several times, but no one answered. He cursed himself as he recalled last night, and the precious little comfort he gave her. And then he wondered if he could ever give her what she needed, whether he would always just stand there, unable to reach out.

When he finally left the development that night, ten contracts for homes had been signed, and there were many additional potential buyers. His builders were ecstatic. But the euphoria he knew he should feel was missing.

Perhaps in gaining what he thought he wanted most, he had lost what he knew he needed most.

Gillian saw the Sunday paper on Monday. She felt joy for Steven, but none for herself.

She had spent Sunday hiking in the woods with Spenser, waiting for the spiritual renewal she always found there, but all she saw was Steven's face, the shuttered look that had closed her out.

He would always close her out. Whenever anything important happened, all the devils inside him would close ranks and shun her.

She loved him, but she knew she also threatened him in some way she didn't understand, and she couldn't live that way, never knowing when he might become a stranger. She would always demand more than he could give. She needed to break it off. Now . . . while she still could. If, that was, he ever wanted to see her again. Which was doubtful.

So when she reached her office Monday and found his call, she didn't return it. She knew if she talked to him, she would relent. His presence was too overpowering, his effect on her too stunning.

She wrote a short business letter, resigning from the account, citing philosophical differences. It would, she surmised, make it easier for him; he wouldn't have to fire her. When she had completed and reread it, the paper was damp from a tear, or two, or three, or whatever, that had dropped. But she resolutely took it to the post office herself and sent it via one-day mail. She also gave her secretary instructions to tell Mr. Morrow she had gone out of town.

Gillian called her other clients and checked on them. She knew she had neglected them badly, and now that the Word Shop no longer had Steven's Cherokee Hills she would have to find some new accounts. What she really wanted was to escape, to run to the Georgia coast for a week, but she couldn't. Not if she continued to have a business. But she could avoid Steven; she knew him, and his pride, well enough now that she didn't think he would continue to call.

She hurt worse than she had ever hurt in her life. Each day seemed endless, each hour a nightmare of loneliness and indecision. Had she done the right thing? But then, she assured herself it was the only thing she could do. For both their sakes. She and Steven were just too different; their needs, other than physical, were incompatible. Still the pain was unrelenting over the next several days, especially when the calls stopped coming. On Thursday, she welcomed her partner back to Atlanta and tried to share in Leslie's joy, but there was a hollow hole as deep as Carlsbad Caverns inside her. She doubted it could ever be filled.

"Russian Circus To Go Home!"

The headlines made the proclamation on Thursday. Thanks to the governor and developer Steven Morrow, according to the story, a number of businesses, including the president of a major airline, had finally raised enough money to send Sergei and his circus home.

She was surprised that Steven had been involved. He never got involved. He hadn't even really gotten involved with her, other than physically. She kept telling herself that. He had never said he loved her, or even cared for her. He had never said anything, for Pete's sake.

Gillian buried her head in her arms and cried

again. She had cried every morning during the past week. She was worse than a leaky faucet. She tried to be happy for Sergei. She hadn't even been out to see him since Saturday, afraid that Steven would be there as he had several times before.

She picked up the phone and called the motel. If nothing else she had to say good-bye and apologize for not going out there, but the memories were too strong, the risk too great.

Sergei finally came on. "We have missed you, Miss Gilly. You have our wonderful news heard?"

Gillian tried to make her voice warm. "Yes, I called to congratulate you."

"Without you we would have nothing," he said. "You do it all. Our animals. Our passage. You must come so we say thank you."

"I . . . I don't know if . . ."

"You must . . . we cannot go without good-bye."

Nor did Gillian want them to. And besides, Steven probably had better things to do tomorrow. Like Cherokee Hills. She had made a few calls to the business editor at the paper and asked them to check on the community's progress. The realty companies servicing it were ecstatic. She felt a current of pride and joy run through her for him. She wanted him to be happy. She wanted that more than anything in the world.

"All right," she told Sergei.

"When? So everyone be here."

Today was impossible. So was tonight. She was

assisting with local public relations for a national rock group appearing in Atlanta tonight.

"Tomorrow," she promised, mentally reviewing her schedule. "Around noon."

"Good," he said with satisfaction. "Saturday, we leave."

Gillian's heart fluttered as she drove up to the motel that housed the circus. It now reminded her of Steven, and the few times he'd allowed her a glimpse inside himself. They'd almost always happened here.

All the way over from her office, she'd remembered the last time she had seen him at the motel, the awkwardness with which he'd responded to Konstantin, the mime. Steven had come on his own then. And that made her wonder whether he might be there now.

But no. He would be at Cherokee Hills, working day and night again. There were no more calls, no attempts to see her. He had obviously reverted quite easily back to type, to the workaholic loner. She hadn't even received acknowledgment of her resignation letter.

The terrible sense of loss filled her again as she parked. There was no blue pickup in sight, and now she knew she had hoped without quite realizing it. She sat in the car a few moments, trying to rid herself of the defeat she felt, trying to revitalize Gillian Collins, optimist supreme.

She looked at her watch. Past noon. And she had

promised. Pasting a false smile on a face that had forgotten how to smile in the past few days, she made her way around the front of the motel to the back where the circus performers usually congregated, where they had practiced and waited. At least they would not have to wait any longer.

The nets were gone, as were the thick pads where the acrobats had practiced. But Sergei stood there, together with Alexei. To her surprise, Sergei was dressed in formal ringmaster attire and Alexei in his clown's costume. When they saw her, Sergei beamed and whispered to Alexei who disappeared.

Sergei gave her his usual bear hug, kissing her on both cheeks, and his exuberance brought a real smile to her eyes. His eyes twinkled when he let go. "My American with the mischievous heart," he said. "Such a good heart. We want all to thank you."

And then they started coming, each performer in costume, one by one in a steady stream, to shake her hand and kiss her cheek, some hugging her as Sergei did, and speaking Russian with accompanying hand and facial expressions, each making himself or herself very clear in their gratitude and affection until Gillian felt her eyes water.

Finally came Konstantin, the mime with the sad, painted face, who pantomimed the story of a circus stranded and rescued as the other performers gathered in a circle. He then blended into the group and another performer, also painted as a mime, emerged from the motel lobby in a loose black overcoat.

For a moment Gillian was puzzled, unable to identify the figure as it came closer, and then the figure took off a top hat he was wearing, and Gillian felt her legs almost give way and her heart thump madly.

The mime had sandy hair and gray eyes that were full of emotion as was the tragicomic face. It was not a stone face now. The paint emphasized an uncertainty and vulnerability that begged to be understood. His hands and face moved in a kind of poetry, saying things he had never been able to say to her verbally, an expression of love and need that reached inside her with exquisite pain, and the wetness behind her eyes formed into droplets.

The figure knelt on one knee and held out his hand to her, and Gillian's heart, which had been beating wildly, seemed to explode with love as the man who had retreated behind so many masks shed them one by one. He was using one mask to tear down the others.

She met his hand with her own, drawing him up, until they both were standing, touching, their hands now clasped together. Their bodies were radiant, heat and light emitting and mixing, becoming one as they moved closer and his hand letting go to wrap his arms around her. She saw his eyes close, those beautiful depthless gray eyes, and she closed her own to block out every feeling other than his closeness, the feel of their two bodies engaging in a homecoming.

Gillian squeezed every lovely emotion from the moment, the safety of his arms, the warmth of his need and caring, the passion their proximity always aroused.

She moved her head slightly upward. "I love you," she whispered, and felt his arms tighten and his body tremble. He didn't answer. He didn't have to. He had told her minutes earlier that he loved her. He had told her in front of the world.

FIFTEEN

Gillian snuggled into the clefts of Steven's body, and her fingers traced the lines of his now scrubbed face.

They were lying in her bed, two sets of animal eyes peering at them, as if incredulous of the scene.

Or so Gillian surmised, because she herself was still incredulous. Steven Morrow was here, next to her.

And he felt so very good.

They had not let go of each other since he had knelt down in front of her. Not even when one of the circus members took their picture, Gillian and Steven standing with the complete troupe. Not when they shared a glass of very strong vodka. Not even when they left, cries of Russian good wishes following them. Not even when Sergei leaned over and whispered in her ear, "He, too, I think, might have mischievous heart."

Steven? It was a glorious thought. That someplace

deep inside, finally ready to emerge, was a mischievous heart, a playful heart. A giving heart.

Gillian still would not let go of him when they reached his pickup, hidden in the service garage. Nor, obviously, was he ready to relinquish her. It was as if both were afraid that, once released, the other would disappear. And so her hand stayed on his thigh as he drove home, and they walked inside the cottage hand in hand. And so he held her as Spenser greeted him like his long lost buddy and No Name peered at him indifferently.

Without speaking, except with their eyes, they went into the bedroom and fell on the bed, Gillian's own face now smudged with black and white paint. They undressed each other, slowly, sensuously, their hands saying what needed to be said, their mouths too busy pleasing the other. His lips trailed kisses down her cheek to the nape of her neck as her hands unzipped his trousers, her fingers caressing his skin as she did so. And then their bodies came together in an explosion of love and need and sensation.

Afterward, he left the bed to wash his face and brought in a washcloth and washed hers, his hands incredibly gentle as they moved along her face. When he finished, he lay back down and pulled her into his arms, and now she was snuggled up inside them, feeling a happiness beyond any she'd known.

Her fingers continued to explore the trails of his face where the paint had been. "I think you missed your calling," she said.

"You do, do you?" he said. "It took me all week to learn to kneel gracefully." There was wry humor in his voice, and Gillian was enchanted, as she always was when he lowered his guard and revealed what he was really thinking.

"All week?"

"I'm a slow learner," he said huskily.

"Yep," she agreed.

"Not that slow," he amended, insulted.

"Ah well." She grinned. "You're cute."

"Cute!" The indignant edge to his voice faded as he nibbled her ear.

"Hmmmmm, very," she said. "Particularly covered with black paint."

The nibble turned into a nip. Which barely covered a low, amused groan.

Gillian's whole body and soul responded to that groan.

She loved him so. She loved him especially now when he seemed so approachable, so . . . giving.

It was as if he knew exactly what she was thinking. His finger touched her nose, drew circles on its tip, but there was a thoughtful look on his face despite the playfulness of his hands.

"It won't be easy, Gillian," he said.

She knew exactly what "it" meant. "It" meant her and him. "It" meant the way he still reserved a part of himself, maybe always would. But he had made a start in sharing.

"I know."

"No, you don't," he disagreed gently. "But it's time that you did."

His hand moved from her face down to clasp her tightly around the waist, as if holding on for dear life. Gillian felt his body grow tense, and she waited, knowing something was coming, something terrible. And it did.

"I killed my father," he said in a low voice, his face now very vulnerable. Vulnerable and filled with a pain she hadn't even comprehended before.

Gillian didn't say anything, just took his hand and held on tight, waiting for him to continue.

"I was from what is now called a dysfunctional family," he said. "Back then we just called it getting the hell beat out of you."

Gillian held her breath. His eyes were now clouded, lost in memories he was so painfully resurrecting. For her.

"You read a lot about violence being passed on from one generation to the next," he continued slowly. "I think that was what happened in my family. My father, after beating us with a strap or whatever was nearby, would forbid us to cry. He was making us men, he said, just like his father had made him a man. But it wasn't just to make us men. He loved to hit. Our mother. Me. My brothers.

"I was the oldest and I tried to protect the others. I was big enough at sixteen to take care of myself, and even threaten my father if he hurt the others, but I wasn't always there. My father had been injured in a mill accident years before and was always home, getting drunk on the little bit of money my mother made and grabbing whichever of the kids was nearest. I kept asking my mother to make him leave, but she wouldn't. Marriage was forever, she used to say, and she didn't know anything else."

Steven, still tense, released a long breath, and then continued slowly. "I couldn't make her leave, and I couldn't leave her and my brothers alone with him, so I stayed, thinking someday football would make it possible to take them all away from . . . the kind of life that fomented violence. If only we had money . . . everything would be better."

"Oh Steven," Gillian said, feeling the pain and tension inside him, part of her wishing he would stop but the other part knowing it was a needed catharsis. When he continued, it was in a harsh voice. "My mother worked at night in the mill and when I was seventeen I had football practice and a job, so Timothy, the brother next to me in age, got the brunt of my father's rage. He was sixteen, and . . . getting just big enough to fight back."

There was a silence, a long sigh. "One evening I was coming home, and I heard my mother scream, and then shouts. My father's and Tim's. They fought often, but there was something different that day. I started running, threw open the door, and Tim was there, pointing a gun at my father who was on the floor, a hunting knife in his hand. There was a long cut on Tim's arm, and blood was everywhere. I knew, by looking at Tim, he was going to fire. I jumped for the gun, and we wrestled for it. I had it in my hand when he grabbed for it again. It went off."

Gillian could see it in her mind. Two terrified boys. A gun. A knife. It was so different from any of her experiences that she could barely comprehend it. Beating small boys to make them men. No wonder, as Robert had said, they all had steel hides. No wonder Steven had learned to hide emotions. She didn't want to cry because she knew it would hurt him. But she couldn't help it. She cried for the boy who was Steven, for Robert, for the unknown boy named Tim. The tears came down her face, and Steven kissed them away. When they had finally stopped, he continued.

"In a small community like Pickens Grove, football is king. Football is everything. The sheriff's kid was my receiver and was, like me, in line for a football scholarship, and it was the middle of the football season. The sheriff called it a suicide so there wouldn't be any bad publicity."

He didn't say it, but Gillian knew Steven had taken the blame for his father's death, the whole blame.

"And Tim?"

"The minute he was eighteen, he joined the Marines. He was in Lebanon during the terrorist attack, and he died there. I learned later, though, that he was about to be charged with beating up a prostitute. Don't you see, Gillian? Violence runs in our family. Before I heard about the charges against Tim, I thought there was a chance we'd escaped it, but then

. . . I realized maybe we didn't. Maybe it was lurking in all of us.

"I had been engaged just before my football injury. She broke it off after she discovered there would be no pro career." He shrugged. "It hurt then, but later I was relieved. I thought I would never marry, just in the event . . ." He didn't finish the sentence, but the words hung unsaid in the air. *Just in the event the taint did run in the family.* "So did Robert."

"That's why you were so surprised the other night?"

He nodded.

"Where was Robert when it happened?"

"Down the road at a friend's house. So was Mike. Both of them kept away from the house as much as possible. But Robert arrived just after it happened and knew everything. He went and made sure that Mike didn't come home. Robert was thirteen and Mike was just ten."

"You said your mother is dead?"

"She died six years later, out of pure exhaustion, I think, just after I started making enough money to move her into a small comfortable house. She wouldn't leave Pickens Grove."

"Robert said you sent them through college? A job you hated?"

"Robert talks too much."

"I'm glad one of you does."

He cocked his head over to the side as if considering her words. Then shrugged as if surrendering. "I wasn't a good student. I spent most of my time on football, and then I had other jobs. I never thought I would need anything but football." He shrugged again in that gesture that was becoming so familiar to her. "But I was injured, and found I wasn't prepared to do anything.

"One of the university trustees, a developer, offered me a job. I was little more than a shill, reliving glory days that weren't glorious at all. God, I hated it. But we needed the money. I stayed with it, baby-sitting potential investors, wining and dining them, picking up a little information here and there but never trusted with doing anything substantial."

Gillian, knowing how reticent he was, how completely private, felt his frustration. She understood more and more Robert's comment: "He's the strongest man I know." No wonder he had so much control. Since he was a child, he'd had nothing but tragedy and disappointment in his life, and yet there was so much spirit inside.

"And . . ." she urged him on.

"After Robert and Mike finished school, I took evening courses in accounting and business. Together with the contacts I'd made with the development firm, it was enough to start a small development, then another."

"And then Cherokee Hills."

"The big dream," he said wryly.

"A wonderful dream," she said. "It's a wonderful place."

"It's a mirage," he said. "It's not the place, but the

people that make a difference. It's taken me a long time to learn that."

But he had learned that, Gillian knew. He had always taken care of his family, even while sealing part of himself away. Because of that fear of violence? A violence she had never seen, even when he had reason for anger.

Instead, she had found a deep core of tenderness she suspected had been within him all these years, afraid to emerge, afraid that it would be weakening.

He had rolled back on the bed, his eyes staring up blindly at the ceiling, as if expecting the worst, that she would be put off by his revelations. She felt a tenderness of her own, tenderness so strong she could barely hold it in and measure it out in a way he would accept.

Her hand went to his cheek and ran along the hard lines that gave it so much strength and character. Now she knew the depth of that character, and felt a pride and admiration that she'd never known before.

"I love you," she whispered.

His gaze went to her face, and Gillian saw the pain and uncertainty there. "I don't know if I can give you what you need," he said. "I don't know if I know how. And I can't promise that . . ."

He didn't say the words that she knew lingered in his consciousness.

"You're the strongest man I've ever known," she said. "Robert said that. I've learned that. You can do anything."

His hand rested on her cheek, where dried tears

remained, making little scars on the soft skin. "You make me believe anything is possible."

"It is," she said, "when there's love."

"I do love you, Gillian," he said slowly, as if the words were torn from his throat. "But I'm not sure I wouldn't end up making you miserable."

She felt the hesitancy in him, the need he'd held so bottled up inside. But he had opened that bottle now and the cork was broken, and he could never entirely seal it again.

"No," she said, her lips touching his seductively. "Unless you go away."

"I don't seem to be able to do that very well," he said ruefully.

"Because we need each other."

He didn't deny his own need. He did hers. "You don't need anyone."

"You wouldn't say that if you'd seen me this week. I was completely useless, cried like a sprinkler system, which I never do, and mooned. I don't moon," she said, indigant at her own failings.

His mouth bent into a reluctant smile. "No, you take life and shape it to your own will."

"So do you," she said.

He looked surprised and started to shake his head. And Gillian understood that he really believed that he had not impacted the lives of others, nor built dreams. A glimmer of light came into his eyes. "Do I?"

"You've certainly taken me and shaped me into something different."

He kissed her softly. "No one can do that."

"But you have," she said. "I never knew I could love anyone this way. And do you know what?"

He smiled at the gleam in her eyes. "What?"

"Sergei says you have a mischievous heart. You just buried it for a while. Konstantin thinks so too. He says you would make a good mime."

"He did?" Steven couldn't hide the slightest hint of pride.

"Do you always answer questions with a question?"

"Only when absurd statements are made," he said grumpily, but with some of the pain draining from his eyes.

"You also have a lovely heart," Gillian said.

His eyebrow went up. "Lovely?"

"Uh-huh," Gillian whispered in his ear, her tongue darting out to make wet swipes across the sensitive lobe.

"I seem to remember being called an ass," he countered. "There's also a lot of that in me."

Her tongue moved to trail little wet paths down his cheek to his neck. "Yep."

"You don't have to agree," he said.

"I don't approve of perfection," she mumbled, feeling his body tense against hers.

"I do," he whispered as he pulled her close to him, and their bodies created a very special perfection of their own. And Gillian found she liked it, after all. She liked it very much indeed.

Gillian walked slowly down the aisle, her eyes turning to the pews, searching for a tall sandy-haired man.

She found him, found his gaze resting on her with a smile.

She smiled back and then continued on down the aisle, followed by the bride, Leslie, who looked absolutely beautiful.

When she reached the altar and moved aside for Leslie to meet her tall dark-haired Scotsman, Leslie whispered, "What on earth did you do to Steven? He's beaming!"

But then all of Leslie's attention went to Connor MacLaren, while Gillian did some dreaming of her own.

The last few days had been wonderful. Day by day, Steven had opened more and more. He was still reluctant to make a full commitment yet, still hesitant about whether he could give her what he said she deserved.

He didn't realize how much he'd already given her.

But he would. He would.

After the wedding he stood next to her in the receiving line, his eyes serious, his smile still too rare, but he'd congratulated Leslie and Connor with real warmth, a warmth that had seeped into her.

Hours later they lay in bed together, and he was quiet. Quiet and thoughtful as he held her. He was spending more and more time with her, as if he couldn't tear himself away, and Gillian took every precious moment and treasured it.

"Leslie was radiant," he said.

"So was Connor," she answered.

"You're going to miss her."

"Yes, but then I have something else now."

"Is it going to be enough, Gillian?"

"Yes." She was absolutely sure about that. Steven would always be enough. Sure, there would be rough times. With his background, with the demons still lurking there, there would be times he would retreat, he would hesitate to reach out, and share.

But he was trying. And he was learning. And she loved him so very much for it.

"I'm not easy either," she reminded him.

His eyes twinkled, the lines around his eyes crinkling. "I know," he said. "You're bossy and stubborn and . . ."

"And I never give up."

"Thank God," he said. He hesitated. That day had taught him something. The wedding, the joy of Leslie and Connor. He wanted it too. And in the past few weeks he had learned a great deal about himself, about hoping and dreaming. And needing. Even giving. "Will you marry me?" The words came out before he could recall them.

It was obvious Gillian was going to give him no time to recant.

"Oh yes, love. Oh yes."

And as she looked at him, at the eyes which were

once so enigmatic and protective, she saw the heart within, the mischievous, giving heart.

And he was seeing the same. His mouth curved in a smile, and he took her in his arms, all the ghosts chased away now by a spirit so strong that he knew he had finally found his home.

THE EDITOR'S CORNER

Escape the summer doldrums with the four new, exciting LOVESWEPT romances available next month. With our authors piloting a whirlwind tour through the jungles of human emotion, everyday experiences take a direct turn into thrill, so prepare to hang on to the edge of your seat!

With her trademark humor and touching emotion, Patt Bucheister crafts an irresistible story of mismatched dreamers surprised and transformed by unexpected love in **WILD IN THE NIGHT, LOVESWEPT #750**. She expects him to be grateful that his office is no longer an impossible mess, but instead adventurer Paul Forge tells efficiency expert Coral Bentley he wants all his junk back exactly where he had left it! When she refuses, little does she realize she is tangling with a renegade who never takes no for an answer, a man of mystery who will issue a challenge that will draw her into the seductive unknown. Hold on while Patt Bucheister skillfully navigates this ride on the unpredictable rapids of romance.

The excitement continues with **CATCH ME IF YOU CAN**, LOVESWEPT #751. In this cat-and-mouse adventure, Victoria Leigh introduces a pair of adversaries who can't resist trying to get the best of each other. Drawn to the fortress by Abigail Roberts's mysterious invitation, Tanner Flynn faces the woman who is his fiercest rival—and vows to explore the heat that still sparks between them! He had awakened her desire years before, then stunned her by refusing to claim her innocence. Join Victoria Leigh on this sexy chase filled with teasing and flirting with utter abandon.

Take one part bad-boy hero, add a feisty redhead, raise the temperature to flame-hot and what you get is a **PAGAN'S PARADISE**, LOVESWEPT #752, from Susan Connell. Jack Stratford is hold-your-breath-handsome, a blue-eyed rogue who knows everyone in San Rafael, but photographer Joanna McCall refuses to believe his warning that she is in danger—except perhaps from his stolen kisses! She isn't looking for a broken heart, just a little adventure . . . until Jack ignites a fire in her blood only he can satisfy. Take a walk on the wild side with Susan Connell as your guide.

In **UP CLOSE AND PERSONAL**, LOVESWEPT #753, Diane Pershing weaves a moving tale of survivors who find sweet sanctuary in each other's arms. A master at getting others to reveal their secrets, Evan Stone never lets a woman get close enough to touch the scars that brand his soul. But when small-town mom Chris McConnell dares to confess the sorrows that haunt her, her courage awakens a yearning long-denied in his own heart. A poignant journey of rough and tender love from talented Diane Pershing.

Happy reading!

With warmest wishes,

Beth de Guzman

Shauna Summers

Beth de Guzman   Shauna Summers

Senior Editor   Associate Editor

P.S. Watch for these spectacular Bantam women's fiction titles slated for August: In **BEFORE I WAKE**, Loveswept star Terry Lawrence weaves the beloved fairy tale *Sleeping Beauty* into a story so enthralling it will keep you up long into the night; highly acclaimed author Susan Krinard ventures into outerspace with **STARCROSSED**, a story of a beautiful aristocrat who risks a forbidden love with a dangerously seductive man born of an alien race; *USA Today* bestselling author Patricia Potter follows the success of WANTED and RELENTLESS with **DEFIANT**, another spectacular love story, this time of a dangerous man who discovers the redeeming power of love. See next month's LOVESWEPTs for a preview of these compelling novels. And immediately following this page, look for a preview of the wonderful romances from Bantam that *are available now*!

With each of her historical romance novels, **PATRICIA POTTER** has won rave reviews from readers and critics alike. Now the award-winning author delivers a powerful tale that proves why *Romantic Times* proclaims her "one of the romance genre's finest talents."

DEFIANT

Only the desire for vengeance had spurred Wade Foster on, until the last of the men who had destroyed his family lay sprawled in the dirt. Now, badly wounded, the rugged outlaw closed his eyes against the pain . . . and awoke to the tender touch of the one woman who could show him how to live—and love again.

Look for DEFIANT in bookstores in July 1995, available from Bantam Books. And in the meantime, here's a sneak preview at this memorable romance . . .

Wade Foster wanted to die, but the devil was being damned unaccommodating.

Wade decided a lifetime ago that living was a worse hell than any Old Scratch could devise. He should have died several times over if there had been any justice in the world. He'd courted death often enough, but then some demon always jerked him back from the final descent.

He stifled a groan now as he looked up at the sun. He might actually achieve his wish this day.

If only dying weren't so painful!

He had two bullet holes in him, one in his leg, one in his gun arm. The leg wound was no problem, except it bled whenever he moved, but his arm was a damnable mess. The bullet had ripped nerves and at least part of the bone. The arm was pure agony and hung uselessly at his side.

Not that it mattered. He was done for. He had no place to go, his leg wouldn't hold him, and he seemed to be in the middle of nowhere with his horse dead.

The pinto lay not far from him. It had been hit in the ambush, and Wade had used his last bullet to give it a merciful death. He'd loved that horse.

But everything else he loved was gone, too. He was used to loss. At least he'd thought he was. He thought he'd become immune to the terrible grief that threatened to swallow him whole.

This last act of his, this final vengeance, should have dulled that piercing, lacerating pain inside that never ceased, not even in his sleep—but it hadn't. Instead victory, if it could be called that, had made the pain sharper because now he had nothing to replace it: no one to hate, no one left alive to focus his rage upon. Only himself.

He closed his eyes, wishing numbness would take over, would wash away the hurt from his body and from his soul. Why did it take so long to die, for the blood to seep from his body, for the dehydration to drain what life lingered? If he had the guts, he'd use the knife to speed the process, but he would probably just mess that up, too.

He'd managed to ruin everything good in his life, from the time he'd stayed too long in town, sneaking a glass of whiskey at fifteen while his family was being slaughtered, to ten months ago when once more he'd indulged a whim while his Ute wife and son were killed. He'd avenged both acts. The last murderer of his wife lay dead just over a knoll.

Wade should feel some measure of satisfaction. But he felt so empty. He had nothing to look forward to, not here on earth, and certainly not where he was headed.

He moved slightly, and the pain in his arm was blinding. It crawled up his shoulder, the way fire consumed dry tinder. Finally, he was swallowed in its fury and the bright scarlet of pain faded into the blackness of oblivion.

"Jake!" Jeff heard the panic in his own voice and tried to control it.

But the wind was blowing hard now, clouds were frothing above, and he'd learned enough about the lightning-quick changes of weather to worry.

"Jake," Jeff called again. The dog had bounded after a rabbit and had been gone an hour. He swallowed hard. There had been reports of a big cat in the area, lured down from the mountain by livestock, and fear tugged at him. He couldn't lose Jake.

"Jake," he called again, and this time was rewarded by a series of barks. They were different from the excited, joyful sounds that usually poured from Jake. More urgent.

Jeff knew he shouldn't be this far from the ranch, not alone, not without his rifle. But then his ma too often treated him like a baby. He was twelve. Old enough to take care of himself, old enough to be called Jeff, like his dad.

The barking became more frantic, and Jeff's fast stride became a lope as he headed toward the sound. That inner voice kept warning him, but he disregarded it. Jake might be in trouble. A trap, maybe. There were still old traps around here, left behind by mountain men who had moved on long ago.

He reached the top of a hill and looked down. Jake was circling something on the ground, pausing now and then to bark again. Jeff wished he had his rifle, but he wasn't going to retreat now. His pa wouldn't have been afraid. His pa hadn't been afraid of anything.

Jeff approached cautiously. Jake looked at him expectantly, ran over to him and then back to his prize.

A body! Jeff hesitated, then took several steps forward. A man was lying on the ground, his clothes covered with dried and congealing blood. Jake sat down, put a paw on the man's shirt as if to declare ownership.

Jeff took another step forward. The man looked dead, but then Jeff saw a slight rise of the chest. He stooped down, touched the stranger's shoulder.

"Mister?"

No response came, not even a groan.

Jeff touched the skin. It was clammy. He looked toward the darkening sky and saw buzzards gathering above. His gaze searched the landscape, then he saw the still body of a horse not far away. He had to get help.

"You stay here, Jake," he ordered, not knowing whether the animal would obey. Though the dog tried hard to please, he, like Jeff, often ignored rules and instructions.

Jake seemed content to stay next to his precious find. Jeff hoped he would stay that way, keep the buzzards away from the stranger.

Jeff started running. Ma would know what to do. She always did.

Mary Jo looked up at the threatening sky and wondered whether she should saddle her mare and go looking for Jeff. She hated to do it. He had reached that age when he still needed mothering but resented it.

She didn't want to be too protective, but she

had lost too much during the past few years to surrender her fears.

She looked toward the mountains. She loved this valley. Cimarron Creek flowed clear and fast several hundred yards from the ranch house, and nearby the Black Mountains rose in jagged splendor. She had been so beguiled by this place, she abandoned her plans to sell the ranch and take Jeff East.

It had also been a compromise with her son. He had fought bitterly against leaving the Ranger station, even more bitterly at the thought of going East. He still wanted to be a Ranger, and though he'd had to leave El Paso, at least he remained in the West and still had his horse and dog.

Mary Jo prayed every day she hadn't made a mistake, that she wasn't risking something more important than this piece of heaven. But it was such a good place to rear a son, open and free. She hoped Jeff would so love this land that he would forget his oft-stated desire to be a Texas Ranger.

Ranching was hard work. But she was used to hard work. She had worked from sunup to sundown at the Ranger station, but that had been for someone else. Now she worked just as hard, but this was for herself and Jeff, and she saw results daily. The garden was flourishing, and so was the little livestock they had.

The one problem had been hired help. The wealth of this land lay in cattle, and she needed hands to develop and run a herd. There were no fences, only open range, and a woman and boy couldn't handle the branding alone. She'd found few men willing to work for a woman who were worth their salt.

She looked toward the hill where she'd last seen Jeff and Jake playing. He had helped her finish mending fences around the chicken yard, and then she'd given him leave to explore with Jake while she cooked dinner.

But he had been out of sight now for a long while, and the sky overhead looked ominous. She was just about to saddle her mare, Fancy, when she saw Jeff running toward her, stumbling as he came.

She knew instantly something was wrong. Jake wasn't with him, and the two were constant companions.

She ran out to meet him, catching him as he started to fall. Winded, he couldn't speak for a moment, then stuttered, "A stranger . . . hurt real bad . . . about a mile . . . north of the old road."

"How bad?"

"He's unconscious." Jeff was regaining his breath. "His shirt and trousers are real bloody, Ma. He needs help bad. There's a dead horse nearby, and buzzards are circling."

Mary Jo didn't hesitate any longer. She couldn't leave someone to die, and she had a rudimentary knowledge of medicine. She'd doctored her share of Rangers over the twelve years she'd been married to one and the two years after her husband's death. She'd worry later about who the stranger was.

"I'll get the buckboard," she said. "You get our

rifles, and that box of bandages and medicines. And some water."

Jeff nodded and dashed inside as Mary Jo went to the barn. She led two of their four horses outside and hitched them to the buckboard. Jeff joined her, placing the medicine box inside the wagon bed along with a canteen and one of the rifles. He held the other rifle in his hands.

"Where's Jake?" she asked.

"He's with the stranger," Jeff said proudly. "He found him."

"This man? You've never seen him before?"

Jeff shook his head.

A shiver snaked down Mary Jo's back. She wished there was a man around, that she had not let the last one go when she'd found him drinking in the barn. The fact was, no one else was around to help. The next ranch was hours away, and the only decent doctor was over a hundred miles away.

Her lips pressed together. Maybe Jeff was exaggerating the extent of the man's wounds. She felt a chill, a blast of suddenly cold wind, and she looked up. The sky was almost black. The storm wasn't far away. She urged the horses to a faster pace, looking frequently at Jeff for guidance. He gestured at a turnoff, and the wagon creaked and jostled in protest as she drove away from the road.

Mary Jo saw the buzzards wheeling in the sky, and she snapped the reins. She heard Jake's anxious bark, then Jeff's cry, "Over there."

She saw the horse, then the man several hundred feet away. The animal was obviously dead, and she gave it scant notice. She pulled up the wagon next to the still form on the ground and jumped down, followed by Jeff. Jake was running back and forth excitedly.

"Stay near the buckboard," she told Jeff as she leaned toward the back and retrieved the canteen.

"But—"

"If you want to help," she said, "get Jake."

"But—"

"Please, Jeff." He nodded reluctantly and whistled for Jake who reluctantly slunk over to him.

Mary Jo knelt down next to the man and felt the pulse in his neck. He was still breathing but just barely. Blood was everywhere, covering and stiffening what once must have been handsome deerskin shirt and trousers.

She'd seen men in deerskin jackets before, but none in trousers trimmed with rawhide lacing. And around his neck, he wore a rawhide string of black beads with a silver eagle inside a seven-pointed star. Mary Jo's gaze moved to his hips, to a well-used gunbelt. The holster was empty, but there was a knife in a sheath.

As her eyes skimmed over his body, she noted the lean strength of him, the corded muscles apparent under the shirt and tight trousers. His hair, longer than what she became accustomed to seeing at the Ranger station, was matted with sweat and dirt and blood. Pain had etched furrows in a face that was hard-looking and deeply browned by the sun. She had no time to notice more. She moistened his lips with water from the canteen, then she shook him gently.

A groan of protest escaped his lips.

Mary Jo swallowed. He was a big man. His present condition did nothing to eliminate the impression of strength. And the two bullet wounds did not recommend him as an upstanding citizen. Neither did the clothes, which looked more Indian than white. Did she dare bring him into her house?

Mary Jo quickly brushed aside the momentary hesitation. He was obviously too weak to harm anyone. She could send Jeff to the next ranch and ask that someone summon a marshal.

Getting him home was the first concern.

She had to be careful. Any jostling could start the blood flowing again, and he had already lost a substantial amount. She checked his arm. The wound was ugly, with the bone partially shattered. Particles of it mixed with the blood, some of it blackened, some glistening white amid the red.

She tore a piece of cloth from her petticoat, dampened it and washed around the wound. She bound it with yet another piece, then bound the arm to his shoulder to stabilize it.

Her attention shifted to his leg. There was a hole in his trousers, but she couldn't see the wound. She took his knife and, with the wicked-looking blade, cut the trouser leg. A quick examination showed the bullet had passed through without the kind of damage his arm had suffered. She bound that wound, too.

Then she eyed the man again, wondering how to get him into the buckboard. She splashed water on his face, tried to jar him back to consciousness, but nothing worked.

She looked up at Jeff. He was wiry and strong

for his age; together, they might get him into the buckboard.

Mary Jo walked over to the horses and guided them close to the stranger. To her son she said, "Help me get him into the buckboard. You take his legs and be gentle."

He nodded. She leaned down, grabbing the man between his shoulders, and lifted. Dear Lord, he was heavy. Slowly, she and Jeff hauled him into the wagon.

"You cradle his head and shoulders," she told Jeff as she lifted her now bloodstained skirt and climbed up onto the wagon seat.

The wind had picked up, chilling the air, and she felt the first few raindrops on her skin. Big, thick, heavy ones. Mary Jo clicked the reins, and the horses started to move. She prayed that the worst of the storm would hold off until they got home. She'd seen these storms before, knew how vicious they sometimes became.

It was the longest trip she'd ever made, each minute seeming like an hour, with the stranger's pain-carved face vivid in her mind. She thought she heard him groan, but it was hard to tell for sure now that the wind was screeching through the trees.

Jake was running alongside, barking encouragement, oblivious to the rain beginning to pelt down, but Mary Jo felt it soak her dress and run in rivulets down her face.

The log ranch house had never looked so welcoming. She drove up to the door and hurried down from the seat to tie the ribbons to the hitching post in front. She rushed back to the wagon bed, wiping the rain from her eyes.

The stranger had not moved. Jeff looked at her with anxious eyes, his hands holding the man's shoulders. "He's awfully still, Ma."

She nodded. She ran to the door and opened it wide, paying little mind to the sheets of rain pouring on the wood floors. Lightning streaked through the sky, dancing in accompaniment to great roars of thunder.

Mary Jo and Jeff somehow managed to carry the man inside and into Mary Jo's bed. He was soaked. His blood was running pink over what remained of his deerskins.

Jake shook himself, showering everything with rainwater. Mary Jo sighed.

"Heat some water on the stove," she told Jeff, "and start a fire in here." She hesitated. "You'd better get the horses inside the barn, too."

Jeff hesitated. "Will he be all right?"

Mary Jo went over to him and placed a hand on his shoulder. It was the only sign of affection he believed manly. Hugs, he said, were for babies. "I don't know," she said. "He's hurt pretty bad."

"I want him to be all right."

"I know, love," she said. "So do I." And she did. She didn't know why this stranger's fate had become so important, but it had. Perhaps because she'd put so much effort into helping him. Perhaps because Jeff had already known too much death. "The water," she reminded him.

She lit one of the kerosene lamps and placed it on the table next to the bed.

Dear Lord, he was pale. There was something vulnerable about a man downed by illness or wounds, especially a man like this. The knife, the way he wore his gunbelt, indicated he was probably dangerous. She had seen enough of such men over the years to recognize the breed.

Who was he? And how had he gotten the wounds? She'd heard of no trouble around here. No outlaws. No recent Indian trouble. She swallowed hard. This man was obviously trouble. And yet . . .

She brushed aside a lock of her damp hair, and drew a chair next to the bed.

She started untying the thongs at the top of the stranger's shirt before realizing she would have to tug the shirt off over his head. She couldn't do that without jostling the wounded arm. She would have to cut the shirt off. The pants would have to go, too.

And then he would have no clothes at all.

She took the knife from his belt, then, holding her breath, she cut the deerskin shirt open. She managed to pull it off the uninjured arm but had to cut off the cloth pasted to the right arm with blood.

His chest was solid muscle, brown and dusted with golden hair that led down to the waist of his trousers. She noticed two scars, one at the shoulder, the other a jagged one on his side. Whoever he was, he was prone to violence.

She took the beads from around his neck, handling them curiously for a moment. They looked like something worn by an Indian, but this man was no Indian, not with his features and that light brown hair. She put the beads carefully down on the table, then turned her attention back to her patient.

Now for the man's trousers. She hesitated. She had seen a man's naked body before, but this stranger was so starkly masculine . . . Even knowing how foolish it was, she suddenly felt very reluctant.

But he was shivering through the wet cloth. Taking a deep breath, she untied the thongs that held the waist of the trousers and pulled them down. He was wearing nothing underneath. Her throat suddenly tightened at what she saw.

Taken as a whole, he was magnificent. Sinewy and strong. She looked at the mangled arm, and thought of the injustice of it, like the marring of something perfect.

She heard footsteps outside the bedroom door and hurriedly placed a quilt over the lower half of the wounded man's body.

Jeff came in carrying a basin of water, steam rising from it, and clean towels. He placed the basin on the table next to the bed, then started a fire in the fireplace. Jake followed on his heels, taking up a sitting position on the other side of the bed, his head resting on the quilt, his eyes full of curiosity.

Mary Jo cleaned her patient's right arm as best she could. She didn't see an exit wound, which meant she had to extract the bullet. Praying he would remain unconscious, she found a pair of tongs in the medicine box and probed the wound.

It started to bleed again. "Keep wiping the blood away," she told Jeff.

He moved quietly next to her and did as she asked. His face, when Mary Jo stole a quick look at it, was tense, and a tear hovered at the corner of his eye. He hadn't realized yet that compassion and being a Ranger didn't go together.

Sweat ran down her own face by the time the tongs finally found metal. She slowly, carefully extracted the bullet. What was left of it.

Mary Jo heard a moan coming from deep inside the stranger, and she sympathized with him. She also felt triumphant. Perhaps now he would have a chance.

She cleaned the wound some more, then poured sulfur powder into it and sewed it up. When she finished that, she sent Jeff out to find a piece of wood she could use as a splint. While he was gone she sewed up the wound in the stranger's leg.

His lower body was covered again when Jeff returned, holding a strong straight branch. He'd whittled off the knobs and rough spots, and intense pride flowed through Mary Jo. Perhaps because of where and how he'd grown up, he often seemed much older than most boys his age.

"That's perfect," she said, giving him a grin of approval. He beamed back at her.

"Can you hold his arm for me?" she asked. Again he moved quickly to her side, doing exactly as she told him, no longer smiling but intent on his job, almost willing the man to survive.

Mary Jo concentrated on tying the stranger's

arm to the splint and then using a piece of sheeting to bind it to his chest.

"Will he be all right?" Jeff asked.

"I don't know," she answered. She finished and stood up, stretching. "But we've done all we can do. If he does live, it's because of you." She gave him a hug and held him close for a moment, surprised he allowed it in his newly discovered need for independence. That he wanted maternal assurance showed the degree of anxiety he felt for their unexpected guest.

But then he twisted away. "I'll get some more wood for the fire."

She nodded and sat back down next to her patient, studying his face once more. The lines appeared even deeper now, his face pasty. His breathing was shallow.

Dear Lord, let him live, she pleaded silently.

Thunder roared, lightning flashed just outside the window. She shivered, thinking how close he came to lying out there in this weather. He would have been dead by morning, for sure.

She rose, lit another kerosene lamp, and sat down next to him.

She had done all she could do.

She could only wait now. Wait and pray.

To enter the sweepstakes outlined below, you must respond by the date specified and follow all entry instructions published elsewhere in this offer.

DREAM COME TRUE SWEEPSTAKES

Sweepstakes begins 9/1/94, ends 1/15/96. To qualify for the Early Bird Prize, entry must be received by the date specified elsewhere in this offer. Winners will be selected in random drawings on 2/29/96 by an independent judging organization whose decisions are final. Early Bird winner will be selected in a separate drawing from among all qualifying entries.

Odds of winning determined by total number of entries received. Distribution not to exceed 300 million.

Estimated maximum retail value of prizes: Grand (1) $25,000 (cash alternative $20,000); First (1) $2,000; Second (1) $750; Third (50) $75; Fourth (1,000) $50; Early Bird (1) $5,000. Total prize value: $86,500.

Automobile and travel trailer must be picked up at a local dealer; all other merchandise prizes will be shipped to winners. Awarding of any prize to a minor will require written permission of parent/guardian. If a trip prize is won by a minor, s/he must be accompanied by parent/legal guardian. Trip prizes subject to availability and must be completed within 12 months of date awarded. Blackout dates may apply. Early Bird trip is on a space available basis and does not include port charges, gratuities, optional shore excursions and onboard personal purchases. Prizes are not transferable or redeemable for cash except as specified. No substitution for prizes except as necessary due to unavailability. Travel trailer and/or automobile license and registration fees are winners' responsibility as are any other incidental expenses not specified herein.

Early Bird Prize may not be offered in some presentations of this sweepstakes. Grand through third prize winners will have the option of selecting any prize offered at level won. All prizes will be awarded. Drawing will be held at 204 Center Square Road, Bridgeport, NJ 08014. Winners need not be present. For winners list (available in June, 1996), send a self-addressed, stamped envelope by 1/15/96 to: Dream Come True Winners, P.O. Box 572, Gibbstown, NJ 08027.

THE FOLLOWING APPLIES TO THE SWEEPSTAKES ABOVE:

No purchase necessary. No photocopied or mechanically reproduced entries will be accepted. Not responsible for lost, late, misdirected, damaged, incomplete, illegible, or postage-die mail. Entries become the property of sponsors and will not be returned.

Winner(s) will be notified by mail. Winner(s) may be required to sign and return an affidavit of eligibility/release within 14 days of date on notification or an alternate may be selected. Except where prohibited by law, entry constitutes permission to use of winners' names, hometowns, and likenesses for publicity without additional compensation. Void where prohibited or restricted. All federal, state, provincial, and local laws and regulations apply.

All prize values are in U.S. currency. Presentation of prizes may vary; values at a given prize level will be approximately the same. All taxes are winners' responsibility.

Canadian residents, in order to win, must first correctly answer a time-limited skill testing question administered by mail. Any litigation regarding the conduct and awarding of a prize in this publicity contest by a resident of the province of Quebec may be submitted to the Regie des loteries et courses du Quebec.

Sweepstakes is open to legal residents of the U.S., Canada, and Europe (in those areas where made available) who have received this offer.

Sweepstakes in sponsored by Ventura Associates, 1211 Avenue of the Americas, New York, NY 10036 and presented by independent businesses. Employees of these, their advertising agencies and promotional companies involved in this promotion, and their immediate families, agents, successors, and assignees shall be ineligible to participate in the promotion and shall not be eligible for any prizes covered herein.   SWP 3/95